Romp

A Steamy Small-Town Romance

Shelley Munro

Romp

Print ISBN: 978-1-99-106323-6
Digital ISBN: 978-0-9951026-8-2

Cover: Kim Killion, The Killion Group Inc.

Munro Press, New Zealand.

First Munro Press electronic publication January 2018

First Munro Press print publication March 2023

For Paul.

Introduction

Give your lover the gift of pleasure...

Gaby Montgomery works for Fancy Free as a condom designer. Recently she's been designing sex toys and testing her inventions with fellow designer Marc, but they've parted ways. The timing couldn't be worse because she's stuck without a willing test subject for her provocative and naughty products.

Gaby's roommates Liam Richardson and Fletch Darcy both want a committed relationship with Gaby, and now that she's free, it's time to make a move. But how do they decide which one will date Gaby? Fletch finally suggests they share her. Liam is skeptical but agrees the scheme might work, which allows Fletch to move on to step two of his romance plan. Fletch doesn't just want Gaby, he wants Liam as well.

The loving is hot, their days full of fun product testing, exquisite pleasure and laughter. Everything is perfect until the outside world intrudes, putting their budding relationship under stress. This time their love and friendship might not stand the pressure.

This is a threesome (MMF) romance. Contains one smart, sassy woman, two sexy men with an agenda, lots of sex toys and a few rotten tomatoes. All's fair in love and war, right?

Chapter One

Country town Sloan, New Zealand

"Quiet!" James Bates hollered the order and waited for the bedlam to subside. All normal for a Fancy Free board meeting. Alice, his wife, winked at him and set down the fiberglass penis she'd been fondling in her hands. Just as well too. He had a devil of a time concentrating when she caressed the demos, and the saucy wench knew it pressed his buttons.

"I don't see why we needed this special meeting." Richard Morgan placed his coffee mug on the table with a thump.

Sam Glengarry, another of the elderly board members smirked, his face lighting with glee. "You're pissy because you'd rather canoodle with Hinekiri."

"Damn straight," Richard snapped. "Shut up like the

man said or we'll be here until Christmas."

"We might as well listen." Joseph Craig indicated the crumb-laden plates in the middle of the table. "The cake's finished."

"I'm ready." Harriet Te Whare's knitting needles flashed like silver swords, yarn twisting this way and that while she completed another row. "Hello, Gabrielle." Her knitting needles ceased their clicking. "Were you looking for me? Can it wait until after my meeting?"

"Hi, Gran." Gaby stepped inside the boardroom and hovered uncertainly.

"Gaby is here for the meeting." James indicated the seat beside him, waving her over. "Come and sit beside me."

She still hesitated. "Should I bring in my bag of stuff?"

James nodded with enthusiasm. "Bring it on."

Gaby disappeared, returning a few minutes later lugging a bulging green fabric bag.

"Do we have a new condom design?" Katarina Wilson straightened, her pale blue eyes sparkling with eagerness. "When do we get to test it?"

The second Katarina mentioned condoms the smart-arse comments and gossip subsided to quiet anticipation. James bit back his amusement. Condoms and the Vibration in particular had made them and the company rich. He couldn't wait to learn what the board made of the product today.

"Gaby approached Alice with this idea last year. We thought her concept held merit and sent her away to develop it into a product."

"What is it?" Ben Kumar leaned forward, a frown creasing his brow. "Surely they can't come up with another condom design? Haven't we done everything? There's ones with spots and stripes, different flavors. They vibrate. Hell, they practically stand up and beg."

Joseph barked out a rusty laugh. "They're no use if something isn't standing."

James ignored the interruption and resulting chortles to continue. "Gaby has developed several sex toys. We intend to choose one and do a Christmas promotion. We'll target the toy as a special gift for the one you love."

"Sex toys are for women," Joseph scoffed. "Stick to condoms. At least both men and women buy them."

James grinned. "Not this one."

"James, perhaps I should explain," Gaby said.

"Someone needs to explain," Sam muttered. "I want to know why we need another new product."

"Hush! That's my granddaughter," Harriet said, the knitting needles halting for an instant while she beamed at everyone. "She's very clever."

"Go ahead," James said drily, yielding the floor to Gaby.

"Maybe you can control them better than me."

Gaby winked at her grandmother and lifted the bag onto the table. She made a show of opening the zipper fastening. Each of the oldies craned their necks, leaning forward for a glimpse of the contents. Her nerves subsided at their curiosity and excitement fizzled inside her. James and Alice had seen her invention and taken one of the prototypes home to test.

"I've worked in the research and development department since I joined the company. I started thinking about sex toys and, in my spare time, I tinkered and developed my own." Gaby pulled out her first toy. "This is a butt plug. It's fairly standard in design. I've made the plug from a material that will hold both heat and cold. Once inserted, the toy will gradually acclimate to body temperature."

Richard winced. "That's all I need. A red-hot poker up my arse."

"Look at Joseph." Katarina chortled gleefully. "He's crossing his legs."

The insults started to fly and, like James, Gaby ignored the interruption to continue with her product description. "Notice the flared base. That's for safety reasons because we don't want anyone having to go to hospital to have an item surgically removed from their rectum."

"I should think not," Richard said in a weak voice.

"We didn't have any problems when we tested it." Alice smirked at James. She let out a sudden *eep* of shock and fell silent, color spreading across her face.

Silence fell and speculative glances winged their way around the boardroom.

"James, hands on the tabletop," Richard said sternly. "This is a meeting, not foreplay."

"Doesn't that depend on your mindset?" Alice asked, cocking her head to the side like a curious cat. "How can talking about sex and condoms all the time not rate as foreplay?"

"Ew," Katarina said. "I don't wanna imagine sex with anyone but my husband."

"As it should be," James said, smirking at Alice.

"James said you'd want to test my inventions," Gaby said loudly. Inwardly she marveled at her lack of embarrassment. Not even blunt talk about sex threw her these days. Not even if it was in front of her grandmother.

Maybe her mother was right and she was a lost cause. No man wanted a woman who always talked about sex or constantly thought about the act. Gaby pushed aside memories of the last hurtful conversation with her mother and older sister because they weren't right. Sex was a normal bodily function, dammit. Nothing to get embarrassed about.

"The secret to any sex toy is to make sure your partner is excited and to use lubrication. Lube is our friend," Gaby said in a firm voice.

"Gaby has designed several new lubes for us to test," James added.

"I'm a fan," Alice said. "We need to market Gaby's lubes. We could give away sachets of gels with the condoms to get people used to using them. You'll see when you test them. The lubes make things nice and tingly. They're excellent."

Gaby couldn't help smiling at Alice's enthusiasm. God, she loved her job. Working for Alice and James was the best job ever.

"What else do you have in your bag of tricks?" her grandmother asked.

"Could you pass these around please?" Gaby handed James several bottles of lube and butt plugs. "I've included detailed instructions with each product plus a questionnaire. If you have any questions you can ring me—not in the middle of the night," she added, knowing her grandmother and her friends too well.

Her mother blamed her grandmother for sending Gaby off the rails in the first place. Gaby didn't want to follow the traditional route of her mother and sister with a secretarial job. She liked making things and she liked sex. Nothing odd about either of those factors.

"This is my second invention and, I think, the best choice for Fancy Free to market. It's a vibrator but different from the norm. I've managed to design a long-life battery that lasts significantly longer than most. I've also made several speed settings because everyone requires different levels of pressure and our bodies are diverse in the way we behave to stimulus. There are five different attachments." Gaby reached into her bag and pulled out a vibrator plus her favorite attachment. "Most of you will have noticed the massage chairs they have at the mall. I've designed this attachment to massage either side of the clit. It gives the most delicious Os." She handed the boxes containing the vibrators to James to pass around. "Make sure you read the instructions. I've tried to keep them brief and concise, but I want to know if you have any problems, either in understanding my instructions or working the toys. I can't correct problems or confusion if you don't tell me."

"Does your mother know about this?" her grandmother asked.

"Nope," Gaby said, forcing a smile and ignoring the tight sensation in her chest. "And you're not gonna tell her."

Ben cast her a sly smile. "Do you still bake those cupcakes? The ones with the pink icing."

"Ah! Good point," Sam said. "How many cupcakes will you give us not to tell her?"

Gaby gasped. "That's blackmail."

"You'd better get used to it." Alice glowered at each of the elderly board members. "They're good at blackmail. It was their misspent youth."

"Where did you get the ideas for your designs?" Richard asked.

Gaby relaxed a little under his kind smile. "I belong to an online group called Romance Divas. We were chatting about sex toys—"

"As you do," Alice chirped.

Gaby laughed. "You have no idea of the discussions that go on in the forum. Anyhow, I asked about the features they thought a good sex toy should possess and went from there."

"I need a sex toy to do what I want when I want," Katarina said drily. "Instead of one that says, I'm coming, dammit. I can't stop."

Sam swept a hand through his grizzled hair. "Huh! You women are all alike. You need one of those genies to keep you satisfied."

Alice's brows shot upward. "Do you have one of those in your bag?"

"Alice!" James said.

She gave a throaty chuckle and the couple shared a private glance that made Gaby hot all over. She wished Marc felt the same about her. An ache sprang to life, her regret like a stab to the heart. Her fuck buddy. The man who'd helped her test countless condoms and new sex toys. They worked together and loved together, except it wasn't love. It was sex. Friends with benefits and nothing more. The day fast approached when she'd have to tell Marc they couldn't sleep together anymore. Her stupid heart had done a number on her and she'd fallen for him, against their rules. She swallowed the knot of anguish in her throat.

Tonight.

She'd tell him tonight, but first she'd have a few glasses of wine to dull the pain.

If she asked, Liam and Fletch, her roomies, would probably go to The Thirsty Cricket with her for a few drinks after work. Then she'd drop by Marc's flat and tell him.

"Okay, that's everything. Does anyone have questions?"

"No, I have to go," Richard said. "Hinekiri is expecting me." He grabbed his sample boxes and hightailed out of

11

the boardroom.

Joseph stared at the empty doorway. "Well, I can guess what's on his mind."

Gaby smiled with the others while inside she cried. At least someone was in for a good night with some hot lovin'.

WHEN THEY PASSED THE three-quarter mark of their usual run along the riverbank, Liam Richardson tossed a grin at Fletcher Darcy and subtly eased up on the pace, slowing to a jog. "I wanted to talk."

"We talk at home," Fletch said.

"I don't want to take a chance on Gaby hearing."

Fletch came to an abrupt halt, wiping the sweat from his forehead and dragging his hand through his damp brown hair. "Am I gonna like this?"

Liam stopped too and turned back to face his best friend. He lifted his thin T-shirt to wipe off his brow. "I wanted to talk about Gaby."

"Sounds serious."

"Yeah." Liam dropped onto a fallen log and stretched his legs in front of him.

Fletch propped one foot on the log and did a hamstring stretch. "So talk."

Liam hesitated and stared at the river, wondering if this was a good idea. "It's feelings stuff."

"No shit, mate. You'd better spit it out or I'm gonna think the worst and you're in love with me or something."

Liam snorted, Fletch soothing his inner turmoil as he always did. "I'm going to ask Gaby out."

"For a date?"

"No to wash the dishes. Of course a bloody date."

Fletch scowled, emotion flickering too quickly through his brown eyes for Liam to read him. Fletch dropped onto the log beside him. "I was thinking along the same lines."

Liam dragged a hand through his disheveled hair. "Fuck. I thought you two were just friends."

"I thought the same about you and Gaby."

"Fuck," Liam said again.

"I've been waiting for her to sort out her shit with Marc." Fletch stood and paced back and forth in front of the log.

"The friends-with-benefits thing?"

"Yeah." Fletch stopped pacing and plonked down beside him again. "What are we gonna do? I'm serious about Gaby. I want something permanent."

"Yep. Me too. Gaby is everything I want in a woman, plus she's always bringing home stuff from work. I'd like to try out her inventions with her. So, what should we do?"

"We can't exactly toss a coin. You sure about this? You're really serious about her?"

Liam stared at his friend and slowly nodded. "I've been thinking about it for a while."

"Why didn't you say something?"

"I'm telling you now."

Fletch sighed. "One of us will have to back off."

They fell silent. Liam stared at the river, watched a stick float past. The last thing he wanted was to fall out with Fletch. They'd never fought over a woman before and he didn't want to make Gaby the first. At his side, Fletch closed his eyes. Despite their dilemma, Liam grinned at Fletch's fierce expression. His buddy always appeared intense when deep in contemplation, his dark hair and olive skin lending him a brooding façade. It gave people entirely the wrong impression of him. Fletch was happy-go-lucky and full of humor. Not much bothered him—he just shrugged it off with his broad grin.

Fletch's eyes popped open without warning. "We both want Gaby, a serious relationship rather than casual, right?"

"That's the way I'm heading."

"We could always share," Fletch said thoughtfully.

A bark of disbelief escaped Liam. "Gaby isn't a piece of cake to cut into equal pieces and distribute around."

"I never said she was. I'm serious about this, Liam. I want Gaby and you want her too. We're best friends."

"Whoa!" Liam sprang to his feet, horror rippling through him. "We're not that kind of friends."

Fletch let the air hiss between his teeth in a show of impatience. "I never said we were, but it wasn't a big deal when we both fucked Jenny May Sergeant. We were naked and we touched each other. You can't help body contact when three people share a double bed. The Earth didn't stop turning because we accidently touched. I felt your cock against mine. You must have felt the same."

"That was different." How the hell had this conversation disintegrated into kinky sex? Kink was okay in its place, but he didn't... "I don't like thinking about you and sex in the same sentence."

"But you like kink," Fletch said slyly.

"So? I didn't see you backing off with Jenny May."

"It was great." A smile full of reminiscence played on Fletch's lips. "What if we could have the same with a woman we cared about? What if we could have that for the rest of our lives with Gaby? Something to mull over, huh?"

"I don't know." Liam gazed at his best friend in bemusement. Why wasn't he smashing in his face? Why wasn't he more indignant about Fletch's proposal? "What about the gossip from the locals?" Shit, he was actually considering this fool idea.

"We already share a house and no one thinks anything of it. We hang out together. Our relationship could change and no one would be any the wiser."

Liam scowled because Fletch made the solution sound easy. "What about marriage? Kids?"

"Marriage isn't as important these days, but one of us could marry her, if that's what Gaby wanted. As for kids, why would that be a problem? All of us have similar coloring. We both have dark hair. You have blue eyes. I have brown the same as Gaby. Does it matter? As long as we all want kids, it doesn't matter who provided the sperm. The kid would be ours."

Sincerity and honesty rang in Fletch's voice and Liam found himself nodding. Everything Fletch said was true, but he didn't believe an alternative relationship would be easy. "What about Gaby's mother?"

Fletch wrinkled his nose. "I say keep away and lock the door if she's in the vicinity. I hate the way she treats Gaby, like some sort of deviant."

Liam snorted. "Good luck with that. At least Gaby's grandparents are awesome."

"Look, we don't have to do anything straightaway. Sleep on the idea," Fletch said. "I'll do the same. If we agree to go ahead, we'll need a plan."

Liam dragged the tie off his hair, grabbed the strands he'd dislodged and refastened it in a ponytail at his nape while he considered Fletch's words. "It sounds cold-blooded."

"No worse than your average courtship. Besides, the three of us could have lots of fun together."

A vision of Gaby came to mind—curvy in a brief red bikini as she sunbathed in the back garden. Immediately, lust swept him, blood flooding his cock and, surprisingly, when he mentally added Fletch to the picture, his erection didn't fade. "I'll think about it," he said finally. "We're not gonna mention this conversation to anyone else, right?"

"Hell no! The only one I intend to discuss this with is you."

"And Gaby?"

Fletch shrugged. "We'll have to manage her. She thinks she's in love with Marc."

"Guy's a bastard."

"Yep, you're not wrong. He's sleeping with Judith Downes. I don't think Gaby knows. I didn't like to tell her."

Liam nodded. "Wise move. Women like to shoot the messenger. A truth bomb would *really* put her in the right frame of mind to consider one of us or both. Hell, she'd probably never speak to us again."

"I never said a relationship would be easy. But Gaby's worth the trouble."

"You're not wrong. You ready to run?"

"Yeah."

They started running along the river trail again, both silent and deep in thought. Liam ran on automatic pilot, his mind on Gaby and Fletch. His friend was right. They already lived together. They rattled around in the same house without any hitches and had done so for the last two years. Perhaps his friend was right and they could take their future into the bedroom—both of them with Gaby.

Chapter Two

"Hello? Anyone home?" Silence greeted Gaby as she shouldered open the front door to step inside the house she shared with Liam Richardson and Fletcher Darcy. Both men were builders and they'd renovated this basic wooden bungalow, adding two bedrooms to the existing one bedroom and office. A large reception room and a designer kitchen, plus a bathroom that was the height of decadent luxury, rounded out the amenities. She'd scored when she'd agreed to move in with them.

She hurried along the passage, her shoes clicking on the wooden floor. In the kitchen, she dropped her bag and the boxes of sex toys and condoms she carried on the counter.

As housemates went, Fletch and Liam were the best. They cooked and cleaned when necessary. Both were easygoing and, despite what her mother said, she'd have trouble finding such ideal roomies from amongst her girlfriends.

She opened several windows and the sliding doors leading to the tiled patio area before scooping up her shoes to carry to her bedroom.

A photo of her and Marc sat on her dresser table—the first thing she saw each morning on waking. Her stomach flip-flopped, her eyes smarting when the snapshot caught her attention. Heck, she wanted to cry now and she hadn't even told Marc they needed to break off their casual agreement. Of course, she could suggest they made their relationship more permanent. Before they started their casual sexual relationship, both she and Marc agreed on honesty in their dealings.

Marc slept with other women. She knew it, sort of accepted the fact. The knowledge hurt, especially since they seemed compatible in the bedroom and at work.

Maybe she should ignore her transformed feelings—the march of lust toward something more.

No, she had to discuss the change of mind with Marc. For all she knew, he might agree to make their relationship an exclusive one.

Worth a shot.

With a trembling hand, she picked up her cell phone and hit speed dial. As she'd suspected, Marc was still at work.

"I need to talk to you," she said without prevarication.

"About one of the condom designs?"

It was obvious Marc's concentration wasn't entirely on her. The vagueness of his voice, the way his voice increased and decreased in volume told her everything. He was busy working on one of his designs. Hope died a fraction.

"No, I wanted to talk about us."

"You want to call our friends with benefits off? No problem. I knew we wouldn't be together for long. You're intelligent and sexy. Someone was bound to snap you up."

A sick sensation filled her stomach at the double-edged compliment. He wasn't bothered. If anything, his voice held congratulation. The idea of not sleeping with her again wasn't even a blip on his personal radar. A tear leaked from her eye and plopped on the back of her hand.

Gaby gathered her pride around her like a protective cloak. "Thanks for understanding." *Amazing*. Her voice sounded normal even though her heart was breaking and tears blurred her vision. "I'll see you on Monday."

"Aren't you coming into work tomorrow?"

Gaby's lips twisted. All work and no play. Deep down she'd known he focused on his work more than her. She hadn't allowed herself to accept the truth, and now reality cut deep. He didn't return her enthusiasm and never would because he was a geeky scientist in love with his work. A handsome, studly one. Although her heart bled, if she stayed in a sexual relationship with Marc, she'd suffer pain a thousand times worse. "I'm taking the weekend off for a change."

"Okay. Gotta go, Gaby."

The phone disconnected before she managed a reply. Slowly she placed her cell phone on top of the rimu dresser. Maybe she'd open a bottle of wine and have a couple of drinks now.

Back in the kitchen, she opened the fridge and pulled out a bottle of Sauvignon Blanc. The front door burst open as she splashed some of her favorite Marlborough wine into a glass.

Her two roomies, Fletch and Liam, raced into the kitchen, panting and chuckling at the same time, no doubt about an off-color joke. They'd already removed their running shoes and tossed half their attire in the utility room on the way past. Now they filled the room with their presence. Their bare chests glistened with sweat, drawing her attention to their muscular builds and their tattoos. Okay, so maybe the scenery wasn't bad around the house either. Her roomies loved sports and rugby in particular, playing for the Sloan first fifteen.

It was surprising a smart woman hadn't snapped up one of them long before now. They both had dark hair. Liam's was black, fairly straight and long enough to tie back at his nape while Fletch's was a deep brown and he kept it shorter. Their builder jobs took them outdoors on a regular basis and helped keep them fit to indulge their love of sports.

Her mother made no secret of her disapproval of both men—uneducated and unfit to lick her feet. Her sister's opinion seemed much the same, although Gaby thought Liam's polite rebuff of her sister's attention several years ago might have something to do with her disdain.

Gaby counted them as her best friends. They'd attended the same school, although they were in Elsa's class and a few years ahead of Gaby. On her return to Sloan after completion of her university degree, she'd met Liam and Fletch in the pub one night. They'd invited her to share the house they'd purchased and the rest was history.

Gaby lifted her glass and hoped they wouldn't notice she'd been crying. "Hey, boys." She let her gaze rove their muscled chests and drifted a little lower, a smirk curling her lips. "Looking good."

"Good enough to run off to Vegas with us?" Fletch winked at Liam. "We could get into some mischief on the strip."

Gaby backed up against the counter when Liam ventured too close. "Don't dare put your sweaty body anywhere near me. You both reek." Her nose wrinkled in exaggeration because they smelled tempting rather than off-putting. If there was some way to bottle the musky, masculine scent and put the aroma into one of her massage oils or maybe a lube, she'd have a big seller on her hands.

Liam nudged Fletch with his elbow, his muscled biceps rippling. "Does that mean I can put my body near you once I've showered?"

Gaby rolled her eyes, half tempted to touch to see his reaction. "Save the flirting for your ladies. Go and shower, and if you're good, I'll buy you a drink at the Cricket."

"You're our first lady." Fletch didn't even crack a smirk when he uttered the words.

"Damn straight," Liam agreed instantly. "I'll take first shower."

"Well, hurry up or else I'll jump in with you," Fletch said.

"I thought I might have dinner at the pub," Gaby said once Liam left. She heard the splatter of water and Liam's cheerful whistling as the ventilation fan exploded into action.

"Sounds good. Can Liam and I tag along?"

"Sure." Relief swept through Gaby. She hadn't wanted to walk into the pub on her own. Not this evening. Tonight she needed fun and laughter. Distraction.

"Great. I'm gonna hurry Liam along. He'll stay in there

for half an hour if I don't shout insults at him."

Gaby nodded and watched Fletch saunter away. *Nice arse*. The words popped into her mind like a magical genie. Her eyes widened and she snapped her gaze back to her wine.

That was *not* a suitable way to think about her roomie.

She picked up her glass and wandered along the passage to her bedroom. The rumble of masculine voices was soothing and familiar. Luckily for her, the guys didn't have dates tonight. They were the diversion she needed to forget her woes. Yep, tonight she'd portray the party girl or die in the attempt.

"What's up with Gaby?" Liam asked when Fletch barged into the bathroom. He wound the towel around his waist and reached for his stick of deodorant.

Fletch frowned. "I didn't ask. I figured if she wanted us to know she would've told us."

"Something made her cry."

"I know." Fletch reached past Liam to turn the shower back on and shucked his remaining clothes to step under warm water that pelted his body from different directions.

The wet room they'd installed the previous year was a

hit with all of them. Fletch studied the waterproof, cream tiled walls and floor, and the single glass screen marking the shower area. They'd added patches of mosaic in shades of terracotta and brown to contrast with the cream. The setup was sleek and modern, with extra showerheads to make the bathroom a hedonistic pleasure.

Perfect for three lovers, he thought with satisfaction. "We should go ahead with our plan. I was thinking about Gaby during the last leg of our run."

"Ah, that explains the smell."

"Ha. Ha." Fletch reached for the soap. "We need to woo her. Get her used to thinking about us in a romantic light instead of friends."

"Yeah like that's gonna be easy."

"Gaby wouldn't be worth the effort if she succumbed without a fight."

"True." Liam opened the door and paused in the doorway. "Okay, I'm in."

"No second thoughts. No problems with me?"

Liam met Fletch's gaze without flinching. "None. Let's do this."

"You shouldn't have forced the last drink on me,"

Gaby said, falling onto their lounge couch with relief. Her legs felt about as steady as a newborn foal's. "I haven't even got the energy to take off my shoes."

"Let me, my lady." Liam kneeled in front of her, his sturdy fingers dealing with the delicate buckles easily. He slid them off her feet, and she let out a groan of relief, wriggling her toes to release the tension in them. Squeezing her feet into sexy red high heels had seemed a good idea at the time.

Instead of releasing her foot, Liam massaged it, digging his fingers into the arch. At the same time, Fletch sat down beside her, close enough for their shoulders to brush.

"Ooh," she purred. "You have magic fingers."

"You learn a lot about massage in sports medicine. We both took a couple of courses along with building stuff," Fletch said. "Anytime you want a full-body massage, let me know."

"So you keep telling me. You just want to see me naked," Gaby said.

"Of course we do. We're male, aren't we?" Liam removed her other shoe, giving her the same massage treatment. The stress melted from her and she leaned into Fletch, letting her eyes close to enjoy the pampering.

"Another drink?" Fletch rumbled the question next to her ear.

Liam paused in his massage. "Do we still have whisky?"

"There's half a bottle of Scottish whisky in the pantry," Gaby murmured without opening her eyes.

"Whisky it is," Fletch said.

The warmth disappeared from her side, but Liam continued his foot massage, smoothing his hands up her calves.

"How come you wore a skirt tonight? You usually wear jeans." Liam's husky voice rumbled through her, soothing and sexy at the same time.

"I felt like a change." She needed something to take her mind off Marc. Dressing to flirt and attract attention helped. Even Liam and Fletch had made a fuss of her tonight—paying more notice to her than they normally did. They'd ignored her sister Elsa and her friends, despite being the same age as most of the single women in Elsa's group.

"You should wear one more often. You have great legs."

"Who has great legs?" Fletch asked.

"Gaby."

"Let me see."

The click of glasses sounded as he set them on the wooden coffee table. Then a hand skimmed up her leg, traveling past her knee and coming to a stop a fraction past her hemline.

Her eyes flew open. "What are you doing?"

"Checking out your legs." Fletch's unrepentant grin echoed in his brown eyes.

"You're touching." Cripes, his stroking fingers were doing weird things to her pulse rate. Belatedly, she jerked from his touch. "That's different from looking."

Liam chortled and handed her a whisky. His blue eyes sparkled as he exchanged a broad grin with Fletch.

"Huh, drink your excellent Scottish whisky." Gaby took a sip and savored the peaty burn across her tongue and down her throat. She leaned back, grinning lazily when the two guys took a seat either side of her. Their shoulders and legs brushed and, for the first time since she'd arrived home from work, she relaxed fully. She didn't have to pretend with Liam and Fletch. They didn't have many secrets from each other.

"I broke it off with Marc." Oops, she hadn't meant to mention this particular topic. She took another sip of whisky. The silence lengthened and she grew increasingly worried about their reaction. She glanced left at Liam and found him grinning. Her brow creased and she turned to Fletch. The corners of his mouth lifted in the beginnings of a smile. "Why are you smirking? Don't tell me you had a stupid bet or something?"

"Of course not," Liam said.

Fletch shook his head. "Why would we do that?"

"So what happened?" Liam asked. "Do you want to tell us or do you just wanna get drunk?"

Gaby didn't want to turn girly on them and start crying. "I think it's best if I get drunk."

Fletch put his hand on her knee and squeezed lightly to grab her attention. "Do you want our company?"

"It's no fun drinking alone."

"I'd better go and get the bottle so we can have refills." Liam stood and wandered out to the kitchen.

Gaby watched Liam leave, her gaze dropping to his butt, outlined in faded denim. Heck, what was wrong with her? All of a sudden she'd developed a butt fetish. It must be her subconscious working on the new attachment for her vibrator. Despite her reasoning, a shiver worked down her spine and a delightful burst of heat hit her lady parts.

"Are you cold?" Fletch didn't wait for her answer but lifted his arm and placed it around her shoulders, drawing her against his body. Immediately heat filled her—a sort of nervous energy. "Anything wrong?"

"No, of course not." Fletch and Liam touched her in a casual manner all the time. They were friends. Their embraces didn't mean anything. The constant immersion in the world of condoms and sex toys had revved her up. The yummy arousal firing to life in her body was hardly a startling revelation.

Liam arrived back with the bottle. "Ready for a top up?"

Gaby held out her glass. It wavered a little. "Oops, maybe I don't need any more. I have to test some products this weekend."

"Yeah?" Fletch squeezed her lightly, drawing her closer.

Her breast flattened a fraction against the hardness of his pectoral muscle. Her nipples prickled beneath the thin silky bra she wore. More thought than substance, the saleswoman had said. She sure had that right. Her bodily reactions were starting to get embarrassing. Right now, what she wouldn't give for body armor.

"What are you working on? Is it top secret or are you allowed to share?"

"It's secret, but the board is testing my products during the next week. If the tests go well and they like them, James and Alice intend to market the favorite one for Christmas."

"That's great, Gaby. Congratulations," Liam said. "We should have a toast."

"Definitely," Fletch agreed.

Liam refilled their glasses and put the bottle aside. "To good inventions and favorable results."

"To Gaby and success," Fletch said.

Gaby grinned, thrilled with their support. "To success."

She'd hoped to conduct her own testing this weekend with Marc's help. Of course now she'd use the vibrator by herself. She probably would have anyway, but sharing the experimentation helped too. "Thanks for being supportive. I appreciate it."

Liam peered at her intently. "Is your mother giving you grief again?"

"Always. I don't let her worry me anymore." At least she tried not to let her mother's attitude concern her. Sometimes her protective barriers slipped and a needling comment rammed through. Gaby swallowed more of her whisky.

They sat in companionable silence with Liam moving only to top up their glasses.

"The bottle's finished," he said.

"Probably just as well," Gaby commented. "I'm not sure how my legs will cope when I need to stand."

"Don't worry, sweetheart," Fletch said. "We'll take care of you."

"Thanks. I didn't want to be alone tonight." She took a couple of sips of her drink. "I'll have to find someone else to help test my inventions. I don't have time to do the whole romance thing." *Cripes. Babble alert.*

"Why does romance have to come into it?" Fletch asked, stretching one arm over his head and yawning widely.

Immediately her hormones hummed to life again. Lord, there was something wrong with her. She wanted to jump her roommates. Either of them would do at present. She wasn't fussy. "Most guys are intrigued when they hear about my job, but faced with the realities of some of the tests they freak. They don't want their performances measured and compared."

"Ah, so that was Marc's attraction," Liam said. "He knew exactly what the tests involved."

"Part of it." She hadn't expected to fall for him.

"You could always let us test some of the stuff for you," Fletch said. "All you have to do is ask."

"I might have, but neither of you has a steady relationship. James and Alice are very careful about security. Besides, I don't want anyone to rip off one of my designs."

"She's telling us we sleep around," Liam said to Fletch. "I think I'm insulted."

"Yep," Fletch said. "Definitely a slight."

"I didn't mean it that way. Jeesh, I need to go to bed." But the idea of heading to her bedroom alone didn't hold much appeal. The last thing she wanted to do was dwell on Marc and lost opportunities. There might even be crying involved. "I don't want to go the bed alone."

"She's propositioning us," Fletch said, nudging Liam in

the ribs.

Gaby coughed. "That's not what I meant."

The guys ignored her protest to smirk at each other.

"Never mind. I'm going to bed." Gaby pushed to her feet and wobbled before staggering two steps.

"Whoa there, sweetheart," Liam said in a rough voice. He grabbed her before she knocked into the coffee table and barked her shins.

She leaned into him, savoring his strength, his warmth and his outdoor scent. The elusive fresh green element reminded her of an amble through the bush and a bright clearing bathed in sunshine.

"You can sleep in my bed," Fletch whispered. "We'll keep you safe."

Chapter Three

GABY WOKE SLOWLY, TOASTY warm and relaxed. At least she hadn't stayed awake half the night, brooding about Marc. Her eyes popped open. It took a few seconds for her to realize she wasn't in her bedroom. She gasped, the harsh intake of air loud in the dimly lit room.

Oh heck. What had she done? She remembered drinking at the Cricket. She remembered arriving home, but her memories were like insubstantial mist once she tried to recall what happened after their homecoming.

"Too early to get out of bed," a masculine voice rumbled near her ear. "Go back to sleep."

She turned her head, shock sending a swift kick to her sex when her gaze met Liam's naked splendor. "Did we...um...do something?" Her eyes roved his bronzed, practically hair-free chest. *Nice.*

"We talked."

"Fletch?" Her snap in the other direction would have put professional soldiers to shame.

"Yes, sweetheart?" He slid closer, his body heat like a sharp poke at her feminine senses. Too close. Wait...

She jerked away in alarm. "You have an erection."

Fletch's brows rose. "Your point?"

Damn, she wanted to take a bite of his pectoral muscle in the worst possible way. She wanted to touch her fingertips to his chest and test the springiness of his chest hair. He looked fine. Sexy even with the sticky-up hair. Her fingers started to itch with the urge to stroke him—his chest, his cheek, his kissable lips. Then she became aware of Liam's warmth searing her back and something prodding her bottom.

A warm hand curved over her hip, holding her in place. She swallowed, instantly sensitive to her return response—the tightening of her breasts that echoed in her pussy. Her breath hitched and she froze, unsure of what to do.

"We're guys," Liam whispered, his breath shimmying across her ear, pushing her arousal higher. "We get erections."

Gaby's breathing kicked back and settled into a choppy beat. The rich rush of desire stunned her. They were her friends. Slowly she turned back to Liam. What the heck had she done last night? She cataloged the sensations skipping through her body and realized she still wore her underwear even if the two men were naked. The unapologetic prod of a cock at her back sent her closer to Fletch.

It didn't help.

The atmosphere in the bedroom—Fletch's bedroom, she noted—pulsed like a live creature. Like a lion preparing to jump its prey.

Jump. No, no, no! Her nostrils flared in alarm, sensing danger ahead. Bad word choice. There would be no jumping of anything or anyone.

"Why am I in bed with the two of you?" Quite a sane question, considering the circumstances, and to her credit, she managed calm when her nerve endings were snapping like rubber bands on speed. *One little touch. One little touch wouldn't do much damage. Right?*

"You flaked out last night," Liam rumbled. "The Scottish whisky did it."

No kiddin'? At least she didn't seem to have suffered more than a fierce thirst for a glass of water and an overactive libido. Perhaps she should've listened to the guys when they'd told her to order the roast beef instead of a salad. The salad hadn't soaked up much alcohol.

Fletch brushed a black spiral curl off her face. That

SHELLEY MUNRO

would be right. Even her hair had gone haywire, the flattening irons she used to tame it, a dim memory. Like her rebellious hair, every inch of her skin pulsed with irrepressible energy.

"You told us you didn't want to spend the night alone." The innocent note in Fletch's voice raised her suspicions. The pair was up to mischief. A practical joke at her expense. Maybe she'd string them along. One thing was true—they'd never hurt her. Both men had proved themselves to her time and time again. The three of them were like family, which was what made her sudden attraction to them so peculiar.

"You promised us a kiss each this morning for keeping you company," Liam said, interrupting her thoughts, his deep voice soothing even as his words alarmed her.

"I did?" She frowned at him while struggling to keep a lid on her intense yearning.

"You did," Fletch confirmed.

They studied her—blatant masculine appraisal at its best. It made her feel hot and cold at once, as if she'd applied one of her test lubes designed to create a perfect O.

"W-what...about...m-morning breath?" Cripes, they had her stuttering like a nervous virgin.

"Don't try to wriggle out of a promise." Fletch tugged

38

sharply on an errant curl. "We intend to have our kisses for behaving like gentlemen."

Gaby sucked in a deep breath, frantically praying for all parts of her brain to start working as a team. *Wasn't happening.* Sensual tension choked the room, making her puddle into a mass of want.

Liam couldn't believe their luck. Marc was history, the field clear for them to convince Gaby to take their friendship a step further. Fletch's idea to put her in his bed and for Liam to join them was brilliant. Undressing had been his idea. A kiss—now that was an excellent ploy. Maybe this crazy plan would actually work.

"Me first." Fletch snared her attention.

Liam watched her eyes widen as Fletch leaned over, pressing her into the mattress with his upper body. Then he blocked Gaby's expression from Liam with his big fat head.

Liam shifted position, craving the visual. *There.* Now he could see the slide of lips, the flash of a tongue before Fletch settled in to kiss her a good one. He heard the needy little sounds and saw one of Gaby's hands creep behind Fletch's neck to hold him in place. Hell, he'd never realized watching Fletch with Gaby would push him this hard. Blood crowded his cock. His hand reached to stroke without permission from his brain. When he realized, he hesitated then gave a mental shrug and continued. If he and Fetch had their way, things would become much more intimate.

Unable to resist, he touched her shoulder with his free hand and ran a finger down her bra strap and over the swell of one breast. Her Māori heritage lent her skin a rich and creamy honey tone. He badly wanted to follow the same path with his tongue and learn if she tasted of honeyed sweet spices. Too soon. Way too fast. He forced himself to halt the impulse.

"My turn," he said finally, running out of patience, and he moved in, angling his head in preparation for their kiss. He grazed Fetch's lips on the way to his target. A jolt of lust struck him, reinforcing the idea that Fetch's half-baked idea wasn't so bad. None of the disgust he'd envisaged eventuated. Score one for Fetch's scheme.

To his relief, Fetch pulled back, clearing his way. The next instant, his mouth hit Gaby's. Soft lips. Sexy lips. He started cautiously, exploring with his tongue, giving her time to adjust to his touch. A shudder rocked him when she took the lead. *Oh yeah.* Nothing better than a woman who knew what she wanted and wasn't afraid to seize an opportunity. Their mouths mated, tongues twining as they explored each other.

If she thought he'd had an erection before, she needed to check him out now. Unbidden his hips flexed, the head of his cock brushing her hipbone and shooting arousal through him. Liam groaned into her mouth then eased back from the kiss to study her expression.

Not a shred of fear painted her face. If anything, she appeared stunned. "Um, I need to go to the bathroom."

"Are you going to come back or run away?" He sensed Fletch's intense interest in her answer to his challenge.

Gaby stared at them. Her tongue flickered out to lick her lips, and she glanced away. "I don't know."

She could run but she couldn't hide. He peeled away from her semi-naked body, rising from the bed to let Gaby escape. She scrambled across the mattress and scuttled from the bedroom without glancing back.

He waited until the bathroom door slammed shut and turned to stare at Fletch. "That went well."

Fletch sat up and adjusted a pillow behind him, the sheet pooling around his waist. "Do you think she'll come back?"

"I honestly have no idea. How was it kissing her?"

"Perfect," Fletch said.

"Yeah." Liam agreed and couldn't wait to do more. His dick pulsed as he visualized running his lips down her neck and taking a nip or two. He pictured faint bruises on her breasts. His mark. Fletch's mark. The intrusion of his friend into his fantasy brought a frown.

Hell, he was truly considering sharing. Sure, he'd said yes, agreed with Fletch to commence their wooing, yet at the back of his mind he'd questioned, worried. His subconscious had bought in, invested in the program already. *Interesting.*

Fletch cocked his head, a faint smile playing on his mouth. "You kissed me too."

"I didn't mean to." Should he admit the physical contact had turned him on? But a full-on kiss with another man... He studied Fletch's face and upper torso in the different light. Speculating. No point going ahead if his body screamed *homo* each time they climbed in bed together.

Fletch's smile faded, his expression intent. Mischief lurked at the back of his brown eyes. "Do you want to try a real kiss?"

"We're naked."

"Your point?" Fletch's gaze strolled across his chest and downward, stilling only when he reached Liam's groin. His erection had faded since Gaby left. Now, to his embarrassment, his cock jolted and started to fill again. Heat built in his face, and he battled the need to cover himself with his hands. He wanted to crack a wiseass quip, but his brain blanked like a fresh piece of notepaper. Not a word came to mind, yet he couldn't seem to resist Fletch's challenging stare.

Without warning, embarrassment transformed to pissed. With two swift steps, he reached the bed and fell onto the mattress. He straddled Fletch, pinning him in place and glared down at him. Part of him expected Fletch to fight. That didn't happen. His friend met his gaze with a mocking one of his own, practically daring him to make his next move.

His head dipped and his lips met Fletch's.

He disobeyed his mind's first instinct to jerk away. Instead, he let his eyes drift closed and pretended he was kissing a woman instead of his best friend. The kiss started out hesitant. They used lips only, starting with the basics. Soft lips brushed his, the faint rasp of Fletch's stubble bringing a difference. Fletch's scent was different too as was his unyielding body, the hard grip on his biceps. The kiss wasn't too bad, and the sky hadn't fallen.

But what would happen if they took the kiss further?

Before he could waver, Liam flicked his tongue along the seam of Fletch's mouth. Amusement bubbled through him when Fletch jerked in shock. *There. Take that.*

Liam started to lever away, but Fletch's arms came around him like bands. He pushed his tongue past Liam's lips and took control of the kiss. Their tongues danced together while Fletch thrust his fingers into Liam's long hair and held on, demanding a response.

The kiss wasn't disgusting. In fact, it was kinda hot. Fletch knew his way around a kiss. He didn't mine for the tonsils, making small forays instead, taking his time and teasing a response, demanding surrender. He shifted closer, aware his erection was a full-bloomed one and there was no way Fletch wouldn't realize.

Sensations unfurled in him, shocking ones, yet he didn't fight. He lifted his hands to Fletch's face and stroked his cheek and strong jawline.

Gradually, the kiss softened and their mouths parted. They stared at each other. Liam didn't know what Fletch saw on his face, but he'd take a bet their expressions would rate identical.

Fletch started to speak but nothing emerged apart from a croak. His throat worked in a swallow then he tried again. "I have an erection. You have an erection."

"Yeah," Liam agreed. "Shocked the hell out of me."

Fletch's gaze was hooded and, despite their long friendship, Liam couldn't read him. "I'm gonna deny this if you ever tell another person, but I want more."

Hell, Fletch had balls of steel admitting that out loud. He could give something back. An admission. "I liked it. Man, I'm gonna deny this too, but you can kiss."

An affronted snort escaped from Fletch. "There was never doubt."

Liam sniggered, rolling off Fletch to lie beside him. Suddenly they were laughing like mad hyenas on a nature show. The release of tension felt great, almost as good as the kiss.

"Gaby didn't come back," Fletch said when their chuckles subsided.

"I smell coffee." Liam fought the impulse to lean over and steal another kiss. "Gaby won't be easy." Hell, where had the urge to jump Fletch snuck from? He felt as if his entire world had tipped upside down.

"Would we want her any other way?" Fletch stretched, the play of muscles in his arms and chest drawing Liam's interest. "What's our next move? Man, stop staring at me. I'm starting to feel like a slice of roast beef."

Liam grinned, despite his discomfit. "You've created a monster."

"I better not catch you ogling my butt on the building site."

A guffaw erupted in him and they started laughing again. Still chortling, Liam climbed off the bed and searched for his boxer-briefs. They were here somewhere. He felt the weight of a stare as he searched but didn't let on. Good to know the curiosity worked both ways. He discovered his jeans and decided to go commando.

"Let's play things by ear." Liam fastened his jeans and dragged a rough hand through his hair, shoving the straight strands away from his face. "Let's get a coffee and see what shakes down with Gaby."

On the far side of the room, Fletch paused in pulling on his jeans. "Yeah, that's what I thought. We might have to start over."

Liam glanced at his friend. "You still want to do this?"

Fletch met his gaze with honesty. "Now more than ever."

A surge of admiration filled Liam. Fletch was one out of the bag—honest. He never told lies, no matter how much the situation might scare him. With Fletch at his side, he could do nothing less. "I feel the same way. It scares the crap out of me, but I don't want to back off."

"Good." Fletch stalked around the bed. He swept him into a tight man-hug, holding him for a few long seconds before stepping away. "I can't always read you. I wanted to make sure we stood on the same page."

"I need a coffee." From the corner of his eye, he noticed Fletch's swift intake of air and the sight soothed his own nerves. On the building site, they made a formidable team, and he didn't see why wooing Gaby would work any different.

They found Gaby waiting impatiently by the coffeemaker. As they entered the kitchen, she removed the glass jug and shoved a mug under to catch the coffee running through the machine. She hesitated on seeing them, offering a cautious smile. "Morning."

"I thought you were coming back to bed," Fletch said.

"Um..." She hesitated before turning her attention back to the coffee.

Liam's gut bucked in alarm. At his side, Fletch caressed his arm, the stroke of callused fingers doing a lot to soothe his agitation.

Gaby swapped the mug for the jug again before venturing a glance in their direction. "I saw you...kissing."

"And?" Fletch asked with remarkable aplomb while Liam's heart stalled in shock.

"I didn't like to interrupt."

"Why?"

Liam was happy for Fletch to handle this conversation. Heat suffused his cheeks. Gaby had seen them and jumped to conclusions. Yesterday, the info would've shocked him rigid too. Anyone suggesting he had a thing for Fletch would've received a quick knuckle sandwich. Now he wasn't sure. He didn't know what the fuck he thought.

"It looked personal." Gaby hesitated, as if she wanted to say more but had thought better of verbalizing her opinion.

"And?" Fletch's dark brows rose in a prompt for information.

"After my initial shock wore off... You looked hot. Okay? I thought the two of you together was sexy as hell."

"Is the coffee ready yet?" Fletch sent him a pleased grin and rubbed his chin. The faint rasp of stubble reached Liam.

"Almost," Gaby said, clearly relieved at the subject change. "I'm starving. You guys want bacon and eggs?"

"It's not your turn to cook," Liam said. "I'll do breakfast."

"No, I owe you guys. You looked after me last night, made sure I got home in one piece." She scowled at her coffee cup. "I don't remember much after leaving the Cricket. Did I do anything I need to apologize about?"

"Not a thing, sweetheart," Fletch said. "Bacon and eggs sounds good."

Gaby poured two mugs of coffee, adding milk and a spoon of sugar to each before handing them over.

Fletch nudged him, and frowning, Liam followed his friend. They parked their butts at the kitchen table, which already bore a heap of mats topped with a pile of cutlery.

"Just move the boxes. It's my work stuff." Gaby placed several rashers of bacon under the grill and turned her attention to the eggs.

"What's in them?" Liam asked.

"Samples."

Liam set them aside, making room for the three of them to eat while Fletch finished the table setting Gaby had started. A well-oiled machine. He glanced up and found Gaby studying them, much like she scrutinized her detailed drawings and plans for her products.

"Something wrong?" Liam took possession of the chair opposite Fletch.

"Yes. No."

"Which is it, sweetheart?" Fletch shot him a swift wink before turning his attention back to Gaby.

"I'm trying to work out if I should ask you something." Gaby checked the bacon and cracked three eggs into the fry pan. With her other hand, she popped down the toast. The scent of cooking bacon filled the kitchen—a comfortable, familiar aroma and one that spelled home to Liam.

"So spit it out," Fletch said. "Maybe we can help."

"Would the two of you help me test my samples?" Gaby turned back to the fry pan and flipped the eggs to cook both sides as if her request was no big deal.

Fletch kicked him under the table to grab his attention. He mouthed something. Liam could only guess what Fletch wanted to tell him. He didn't care since Gaby had offered them a way to get close to her.

"What would the tests involve?" Fletch took a sip of his coffee. He was playing it cool, but Liam noticed the small boy inside his friend leaping for joy.

"Sex."

Liam almost spat out the coffee he was trying to swallow. God, he loved a blunt woman.

"What sort of sex?" Fletch shot him a scowl, warning him to cool it.

Liam took the point and sobered immediately. Fletch was right. Gaby seemed skittish about the idea. He'd hate her to rescind the offer. No, they needed to lull her suspicions.

"Well, the two of you could..." She trailed off, her hand gesturing toward them.

"Fletch dared me to kiss him," Liam said, straining to keep the defensive note from his voice. *No. No. No!* As much as he'd enjoyed kissing Fletch, they both wanted Gaby. This plan of theirs was gurgling around the toilet bowl, ready to flush away. They had to convince Gaby they required her presence in testing her products.

"It's true," Fletch said. "I dared him."

Gaby's brow wrinkled and she turned to them, toast slice in hand. "Maybe we could test my samples together." She spoke rapidly, as if worried about the content of her thoughts.

Fletch set down his coffee and absently clunked a teaspoon against the side of the sugar bowl. "The three of us?"

"I guess it's a bad idea," Gaby said, apologetic. "Forget I mentioned it."

Panic filled Liam. At this rate, Gaby would talk herself out of the suggestion before they agreed. "You took us by surprise because you've always kept your work secret from us before. Nothing wrong with your idea." Did he sound excited? Too eager?

"You'd consider it?" Gaby kept her back to them while she served the food.

Liam exchanged a speaking glance with Fletch. *What should we do now?*

Luckily Fletch read his mind exactly. "Gaby, of course we'd like to help you, but we need to discuss the situation first. We'd hate sex to fuck up our friendship."

Gaby picked up two plates and strolled over to the table. She set one plate in front of each of them before returning to collect hers and the rack of toast. "More coffee?"

"Sit. I'll grab the coffeepot." Liam sprang to his feet and returned to the table with both the coffeepot and the milk.

"I'm sorry. I shouldn't have suggested testing with you guys. You're right, of course. I was wrong to spring the idea on you."

"Gaby, shut up," Fletch said in a kind yet determined tone. "Give us a chance to speak for ourselves."

She pressed her lips together until they practically disappeared, making her look like a prim maiden aunt. After leaving them, she'd taken the time to comb her hair and clean off the makeup she'd worn the previous evening. God, she was beautiful. Liam's heart hurt every time he looked at her. She kept her black hair long and it had a natural curl, twirling into cute spiral curls that called out for tugging. Sometimes she straightened her hair, but he liked it this way best—wild and free. She took after her European father most, but she had a lot of her mother in her too.

He'd bet she'd received her love of life from her grandmother. Harriet Te Whare was a wonderful woman, and he and Fletch adored her. During their teen years, they'd spent many hours at Gaby's grandparents' farm, either riding horses or swimming at the river.

"We don't want to spoil our friendship either. I can't speak for Liam, but I'm not dating anyone at present. I'd like to help with your testing. Truth is, I'm dying to learn more about your work. You're always closemouthed about your experiments. I'd enjoy helping you."

"I'm in," Liam said. "I'm not seeing anyone either.

Besides, we've known each other for a long time. We're helping you with your work. Why would that cause problems? Hell, Fletch and I kissed this morning. We're still talking."

"Are you going to kiss again?"

Fletch shared a swift glance with him before turning back to Gaby. "You want to know because?"

"I want to watch."

Chapter Four

GABY DREW A SHARP breath, aghast at her words. The truth was she'd frozen on seeing the two men kiss. Shock had yielded swiftly to surprise and speculation. They'd appeared comfortable, focused solely on each other.

A part of her had envied their closeness. Marc might have enjoyed the sex with her, but it was never totally about pleasure. Their coupling was always about the condoms. How did they fit? How did they feel? Did they perform to expectation? Did they need a different scent or should they tweak the design?

Sex with Marc was business, on his side at least. Part of her still ached to pick up the phone and ask him to continue with their friends-with-benefits deal.

"Gaby?"

"What?" Oops, she'd zoned out on them. "If you're that relaxed with each other you're naturals for helping me to test my sex toys. Besides, neither of you seemed to have a problem with kissing me. I figured the actual sex part wouldn't create a problem either."

"What about the risk of pregnancy?" Liam asked.

Gaby sent him a look of approval. "It's always possible one of the condoms might break because they *are* test models. We do tests with machines first before we use people, but I'm on the Pill just in case. I take regular physicals and I'm clean."

"Liam and I had blood work done last month. They tested for everything."

"How come you had tests? You never mentioned them," Gaby said, diverted from her worries.

"Our rugby coach wanted to check our end-of-season fitness levels. The sports medicine department at the university where his daughter works needed volunteers so they worked a trade. They poked and prodded us for an entire weekend," Liam said. "You were concentrating on a work project at the time."

"Oh. Okay." Gaby buttered a piece of toast and cut it in two. "Do you guys have any plans for the rest of the weekend?" She cringed inwardly, knowing she might come across as sex-starved. "The testing is time-sensitive. I need at least some results this weekend so I can work on finessing my design. James and Alice want to market the chosen product during the run-up to Christmas. Christmas is coming so I need to get a move on with the testing. I..." She trailed off, aware she'd lost them somewhere. They were staring at each other with wide eyes. *Shock.*

Heck, she'd traumatized them with her blunt demands.

"Christmas is *coming*?" Liam exchanged a glance with Fletch. His lips quivered and seconds later, he exploded into laughter. He fell against the table, almost toppling off his seat.

"What?" Gaby didn't have to pretend confusion.

"You've found your marketing angle," Fletch said with another guffaw. "That's a perfect slogan for a sex toy. All going well, everyone will come."

"Oh! Brilliant." Gaby flashed them an excited grin. "Why didn't I think of that before? I'll tell James and Alice on Monday. Hopefully by then I'll have a better idea which toy we'll market."

"Are we allowed more details?" Liam asked.

Gaby tossed them an uncertain look. "Either of you have experience with anal sex? Some guys are a bit squeamish about anything outside the bounds of traditional." She found herself tensing, waiting for their reply. *Please say you're okay with this.* Testing on her own wouldn't be much fun, and she hated to dwell on Marc. Having Fletch and Liam around would distract her.

"Anal sex is fine," Liam said.

"Have you...um...with each other?"

"Not yet," Fletch said.

Mid-swallow, Liam let out a peculiar choking croak and Fletch clapped him over the back.

"Fuck, don't say things like that when I have a mouthful," Liam said once he could breathe again.

"So you're okay with kinky?"

"We're willing to try anything you throw at us. Right, Liam?"

Liam shot Fletch a swift glare before turning back to her. "If there's something we're not happy about, we'll let you know. Will that work?"

"Perfect."

"Fletch and I need to check on the building site, but we'll be back midmorning. Is that okay?" He glanced at Fletch again, and the two seemed to communicate without words.

"I'll get everything ready. I wanted to sort out the paperwork anyway."

"Did you see Suzy Richards last night?" Fletch asked, changing the subject.

"She wandered her hands all over Jeremy Collins, the guy from the Children of Nature cult," Liam said.

"Doesn't he already have a woman?"

Gaby relaxed into their local gossip with relief. "Last time I saw her she was heavily pregnant. I wonder if Suzy realizes she'd be woman number two or even three."

Five minutes later, the two men left. A low-level thrum spiked in her pussy and she shuffled around on her chair, tightening her thighs to coax out more of the sensation. Magic pulsed in the air or at least—she hoped it was enchantment. The more she considered her suggestion, the better the idea sounded. This wasn't a mistake. She valued their friendship. The last thing she wanted was to find somewhere else to live.

Kissing Liam and Fletch this morning had revved her motor. She couldn't wait to see how they dealt with her sex toys.

FLETCH FOLLOWED LIAM FROM the house, waiting until they were far enough away before demanding, "What the fuck are we doing? There's no pressing need for us to visit the site today. What if Gaby has second thoughts about this while we're away?"

"We need to talk over what we will and won't do."

A quiver of anticipation rocked Fletch. He knew where

his boundaries lay, but perhaps Liam was right. It was better to discuss this away from Gaby. "Fair enough. We might as well check the progress on the site. Are we going in my vehicle or yours?"

"Mine is pointing in the right direction." Liam fished his keys from his jacket pocket. "Do you think Gaby will change her mind?"

"Knowing Gaby, no. She seemed...I dunno...excited."

Liam unlocked his SUV and jumped behind the wheel. "That's what I thought."

"So what's your problem?" Fletch liked confronting things, demanding answers in order to plan ahead. This topic fell into the category of strategic planning. Six months ago, almost to the day, he'd looked at Liam and realized he'd wanted more from him than friendship. The idea shocked the hell out of him at first. He'd seen Liam with a woman—Jenny May—and jealousy hit him over the head. They'd ended up fucking her together and it had turned into one of the most satisfying sexual encounters in memory. After much thought, he'd realized Liam's presence made the difference. He'd enjoyed the surge of cock against his own, hadn't minded the closeness or intimacy with another man because it was Liam.

"I wanted to know how far you're willing to go."

Fletch frowned. "What do you mean?" The jealousy

he'd experienced when Liam hooked up with Jenny May hadn't been because of a woman.

Gay.

He'd worried for about two seconds. He enjoyed fucking a woman, yet the experience improved a hundredfold with Liam. He'd done some online research and emerged enlightened and a bit disturbed. A few sleepless nights and he'd reached a decision. He wasn't gay but he was attracted to Liam.

He had to tread carefully.

Liam's confession about his feelings toward Gaby offered an opportunity, one too good to pass up. His two favorite people in bed with him. Nope, only an idiot would turn down a chance like this.

"When Gaby was talking about anal sex, I don't think she meant just with her. She meant us having sex with each other."

"That worries you?" Fletch sneaked a glance at Liam. He didn't appear distressed. *Yet.*

Liam concentrated on the tarmac. Not that Sloan traffic clogged the roads or anything. "I don't know what to friggin' think. It feels as if this sex thing is spiraling out of control and we haven't done anything yet."

"We don't have to do anything."

"I want to do this." Liam's smile was rueful. "I'm willing

to do anything. I don't think I'll even hesitate at kinky because it's you and Gaby."

Something twisted inside Fletch at Liam's words. The ball of tension in his gut dispersed. "That's what I was thinking. It's not as if any of us would gossip. I trust you and Gaby. I thought I'd approach this with an open mind."

"We might be overanalyzing the situation anyway," Liam said, taking a right turn onto Marchant Road.

They passed two paddocks of Hereford cattle with their distinctive chestnut-colored bodies and white faces. Three horses and a paint pony grazed in the corner paddock where he took another right onto Davies Road. The building site was at the end of the road, a huge mansion of eight bedrooms, two reception rooms, luxury kitchen plus a wine cellar, gym and indoor pool. The customers expected the best and willingly paid for materials of the highest quality. The building was a joy to work on, especially with Liam at his side. They both relished building things and worked together well. Hopefully this would extend to loving Gaby.

NERVES STUTTERED THROUGH HER the entire morning, only increasing when a vehicle pulled up outside the house.

They were back. Did she want to go ahead with this? She paused a beat. *Hell yeah.* Imagining the two of them naked and at her disposal had her wet enough to start right now. No need for foreplay, that was for sure.

"Hey," she said, striving for casual and friendly when they walked—no prowled—into the kitchen. Two dangerous, sleek cats. Inwardly, she scoffed at her thoughts. Her mother always said her reading material helped to push her onto the path to ruin.

"Smells good." Liam came to a halt. "I thought it was my turn to cook."

"So you keep saying. I made a casserole. Dinner can cook, leaving us free to do other stuff."

"At least she's feeding us," Fletch said. "We should give thanks."

"Fletch!" Cripes he made it sound as if she was forcing them into slavery. Her gaze roved their chests. Both were equally attractive and muscular from physical work and sports. "You would make excellent slaves. I do like to eat grapes."

"We'll peel your grapes anytime," Liam said.

Fletch chuckled. "We're looking forward to this. I can't wait to play with your inventions."

His comment prompted a question. "The pair of you

speculate about my work?"

"Of course we do," Liam said. "Hell, most of the single men and half the married ones wonder what you guys get up to at Fancy Free."

"I bet." Gaby patted the focaccia bread dough. "I've heard every suggestive come-on line in the book."

"Not from us," Fletch protested.

"No, thank goodness. It's earned you guys a ton of points. I'm nearly done here. I'll finish off the bread and leave it to rise." She tossed a grin at them. "Don't start without me. If there's any kissing, I want to watch."

"We're men. We do everything in a hurry," Fletch said.

She winked. "Not everything, according to Jenny May."

"And they accuse men of gossip." Liam shook his head and departed in the direction of the bedrooms. Once again, her gaze drifted to his backside, faithfully outlined in faded denim. But this time Fletch caught her.

He waited until Liam disappeared from sight. "My arse is better."

"Says who?" Liam shouted.

"Damn, I didn't think he'd hear."

Gaby chuckled. "Take the boxes to the bedroom for me."

"We'll be in my room since it's biggest." He picked up the boxes she'd indicated and left the kitchen.

"Don't peek inside." Gaby sighed as she stared after him. Fletch's butt was pretty spectacular, but choosing one over the other? They both looked tasty. She finished the bread dough and set it aside in a warm spot to rise. She cleared the counter and wiped it down then looked for something else to clean. Oops! Stalling. Once she realized she was guilty of dithering, her stomach did a distinct somersault. Nerves. Taking a deep breath, she wiped her hands on a towel and marched to Fletch's bedroom.

Gaby wasn't sure what to expect when she entered the bedroom, but it wasn't two men discussing size.

An intoxicating giggle tickled the back of her throat and she struggled to keep it under control. Giggling Gertie wasn't the impression she wanted to make. "Is it true there's a correlation between foot size and cock length?" She managed to get the words out without chortling. They started like two guilty boys, playing with things they shouldn't.

"We peeked in the box," Fletch admitted.

Liam tossed a boyish smile in her direction. "And got sidetracked by the condom sizes."

Gaby's mouth twitched. "So you decided to whip them out and compare."

"Of course." Liam's gaze dropped from her face to her breasts. "Don't women compare their breasts?"

"Um, no. Not really."

"Well, there goes that fantasy," Fletch said.

"What do we get to try first?" Liam asked.

"I need to test these condoms." Gaby plucked a box from Liam's hands. "They're a new one we're experimenting with. Most of our rival companies are doing something similar and coming up with ultra-thin condoms. We're aiming for a product that feels natural, almost as if you're not wearing a condom at all." Gaby grabbed her clipboard from inside the box along with a pen. "I need my glasses. Won't be a sec. Don't lose those erections, boys."

"As long as she doesn't whip out a tape measure," Fletch said.

She didn't catch Liam's reply, merely heard the masculine rumble when she grabbed her reading glasses off the dresser top. She also picked up a scrunchie and pulled her hair in a ponytail before hurrying back to join the men. She came to a halt in the doorway, a soft breath hissing out.

This time they were lying on the bed, arms wrapped around each other as they kissed. Enthralled, she watched them experiment. It was obvious from their cautious proceedings they hadn't done this much, although why they were doing it now escaped her. But it was hot watching their big hands clutching each other, their mouths crushed together. Oh yeah. She fanned the heat from her face and stepped farther into the master bedroom.

Like the rest of the house, the two men had decorated this room with style. Not your typical bachelor establishment. Three walls were painted cream—a sort of a French vanilla color—while they'd made a feature of the remaining wall, papering it with patterned wallpaper. Twists of subtle vines and leaves covered the wall and they'd pulled the effect together by using the chocolate brown, green and cream of the wallpaper with the other furnishings.

The sturdy wooden king-size bed dominated the room. Sliding doors connected the room with the garden and there was an en suite, although Fletch preferred the main bathroom with its huge, open wet room area. Gaby preferred it too with the double showerheads and efficient ventilation system that meant she could shower and apply makeup in the one place.

A moan escaped one of the men and Gaby smiled. Time to interrupt their kissing otherwise they'd never get anything done. "Hey, couldn't you have kept your erections by using your own hands?"

They parted like a pair of newly released springs. A trace of red appeared on Liam's face while Fletch stared at her without inflection.

"He dared me," Liam blurted.

Her brows rose and she sauntered up to the bed. "Do you accept all his dares?"

The two men exchanged a smirk. "Pretty much," Liam confessed. "He's a bad influence."

"Yeah, right. I broke my arm when I jumped off the roof dressed as Superman. Your idea," Fletch countered.

"Okay." Gaby picked up her clipboard before grabbing two sample condoms. "I want to test these unfurl properly and also fit."

"You're gonna touch our dicks?" Liam asked, frowning.

"That's the usual way sex goes," Gaby said. "Parts touch and create friction. I want to make sure the contact is the good kind. Who's first?"

"I'll go first," Fletch said. "What happens if I get a bit enthusiastic?"

"You should know how to hold your shit together by now," Liam said, challenge in his deep tones. "We can always bet on who loses control under Gaby's skilled hands first."

Gaby snorted and consulted her clipboard.

"She reminds me of a prim schoolmistress when she wears her glasses," Fletch said.

"'She is in the room with you.' Gaby handed her

clipboard to Liam. "Move over so I can straddle Fletch's legs." This situation was something she'd never imagined in all their years of friendship, yet it didn't feel wrong. Her instincts weren't screaming at her to run in the opposite direction and spending time with Liam and Fletch was taking her mind off Marc.

Bother, she hadn't meant to think about him. She wouldn't. "Are you ready for me to touch you?"

"Hell yeah."

"Then why do you look so nervous?" Liam's gaze held distinct challenge.

"You're both staring at my cock. I'm starting to feel self-conscious."

"I'll make it quick and painless," Gaby promised, trying not to snicker at the caution on his face. "Liam, write this down for me please. Sample BCD5." She knew the perfect way to reward him. "I'm going to touch you. Okay?"

"Yeah." Fletch didn't sound too confident.

She wrapped her hand around his cock and stroked him, watching his face carefully at the same time.

"Fuck," Fletch said, arching up into her grip.

Gaby continued for several more strokes, letting him become used to her touch. She made a *tsking* sound. "Guys are so easy."

"We like sex," Liam said. "Nothing wrong with that."

He watched the glide of her hand—up and down, up and down as if mesmerized.

Fletch glared at her when she stopped the motion. "I was enjoying that."

"Patience, grasshopper." Gaby slipped the condom from the sealed wrapper and popped it between her lips. She sensed the guys' shock but concentrated on the condom and the taste. Not bad. At least it didn't have the rubbery, latex-type taste many condoms held. She'd managed to get that right. Bending over Fletch's groin, she held his cock in one hand and, using her mouth and lips, rolled the condom into place.

"Wow, that's a talent, Gaby." Fletch sighed his pleasure, moaning when she applied suction. "Man, you should feel the heat from Gaby's mouth. The latex doesn't deaden sensation much."

Gaby gave him one final swipe, part of her wishing she could taste him instead of the condom. She lifted her head and winked at Liam. "That's one tick for the chart."

"Why are we testing condoms first? I thought you wanted to trial sex toys," Liam said.

"Liam, can you note down the latex tastes okay and there's no appreciable loss of sensation." Gaby turned to Fletch. "Any other comments to add?"

"Yeah, can we move this along?"

Gaby ignored his complaint. "My thoughts were these ultrathin condoms form part of a package especially for Christmas. A package for lovers or for the one you love. The condoms would be in red and green. A bottle of the lube would be included plus the sex toy with the basic attachment. The other attachments come as extras and can be purchased separately."

Fletch rolled his eyes. "Great. She's gonna make the dicks of New Zealand men look like candy canes." He was only pretending affront, teasing as usual.

"You guys have themes in your decorating," Gaby said.

"Why would we care if we're gonna get off?" Liam checked the clipboard and jotted down the points she'd mentioned. "What's next?"

"Your turn." Gaby plucked another condom from her box.

"Let me," Fletch said.

Gaby stared at Fletch before turning to study Liam. "What's going on with you two today?"

"Gaby can do it," Liam said.

"Aw, you're hurting my feelings."

A tic sprang to life in Liam's jaw. His eyes narrowed on Fletch and he wasn't smiling. "Gaby can do it."

Fletch did laugh, as if he were joking, but she caught a hint of hurt on his face before his normal good humor slid into place.

Gaby climbed off Fletch and moved across the bed to where Liam was standing. He'd lost all trace of an erection. She climbed off the bed and kneeled in front of him. Something was definitely going on between the boys. Twice, she'd watched them kiss and they'd both appeared into the intimacy. Having her as a buffer might help them find each other, make them more willing to adventure into the taboo area of sex between two men.

If exploration was what they wanted.

She lifted her head and licked down his flaccid cock. Her fingers stroked his balls while she nibbled his abdomen and teased him. His musky outdoor scent filled every breath as she explored him. To her relief, he responded quickly to her ministrations. She licked the length of his cock again, doing a teasing pass over the ruddy crown. When a drop of pre-come beaded at his slit, she licked it clean. Slowly, she pulled away and rocked back on her heels to glance up at him. "Okay?"

"Yeah." It was a husky sound. "More?"

Gaby grinned and reached for the condom. "I'll do my mouth trick another time. I want to check the fit as I roll the condom on for you."

This condom was a leafy green. A grin formed as she rolled the latex down the length of his penis.

Fletch let out a snigger. "He looks like an alien."

"I wouldn't cast stones if I were you. You're sporting a candy cane."

"Stop bickering," Gaby said. "Okay, how does that feel? How does this condom stack up against the ones you're using at the moment?" She paused to take Liam into her mouth to let him feel the heat of her mouth through the latex. She licked and sucked until a tremble racked him. His cock lengthened even farther, and a second tremor worked through his muscular body. His hands drifted down to cup her skull, holding her in place and tugging at her hair. A surge of lust speared through her at his rough handling. Liam was always a little quieter than Fletch and not as outgoing. His urgency both surprised and pleased her.

It told her the sex between them would be hot, more than mere testing of Fancy Free products. Her stomach tightened as she hummed around his shaft, taking the teasing up a notch. With a final lick, she fought his grip and pulled away the instant he released her.

She grinned up at him. "How is the condom?"

"Great," Liam said. "Almost as if I'm wearing nothing."

"How robust are they?" Fletch asked from where he reclined on the bed.

"That's what we're about to find out. On the bed."

"She's ordering us around," Fletch said.

Gaby turned away to hide her smile and pulled out a plain plastic bottle of lube. One of her inventions. The vibrator came out next along with a bag of attachments. She extracted the basic one and clicked it into place. Then, with a deep breath to help contain the renewed burst of nerves, she stripped off rapidly, returned to the bed and crawled between the two men.

"Pretty," Fletch said, openly admiring her figure.

She handed her precious vibe and the lube to Fletch, waiting in clear expectation for him to switch on the toy or ask questions.

"You expect us to start straightaway? Don't we get hands-on privileges?" Liam asked. "You checked us out."

Gaby controlled her blush with difficulty, she who seldom blushed. "You'll be touching me." A surge of excitement pulsed inside her, the pressure of arousal sliding through her lower body. Somehow, she didn't think she'd need the lube.

"I can't decide where to touch first. You're beautiful, Gaby." Liam's gaze was like the warm stroke of fingers as he studied her.

"You've seen me in a bikini."

"Yeah, but we didn't get the full effect," Fletch said, setting her vibrator and lube aside.

Gaby raised her brows, valiantly attempting to control the escalation of arousal. She wanted to jump them. She dampened further, turning liquid deep inside at the idea of them jumping her.

Liam waded in with his opinion. "Gaby, we're guys. We see a beautiful woman and we wonder. It's our nature."

"So you keep saying. Let's get started. I've clicked the basic attachment on for you. Check to see if the removal is instinctive. Tell me what you think of the workmanship. Is it robust enough? I'd like to discover if you guys can work the vibrator and the attachments without me giving you instructions."

Fletch waggled a forefinger at her in a chiding manner. "You can't expect us to jump right into sex without any foreplay. I thought women liked foreplay."

"But this isn't regular lovemaking," she protested.

"Aren't we meant to be simulating the real thing?" Fletch shot back.

His logic took her aback. She was offering no-strings sex where they didn't have to romance her or exert themselves much in the way of foreplay. All she required was a body to do what she requested when she demanded. Having two such bodies at her disposal was a bonus, but she hadn't expected them to prove difficult. Men liked sex and were like dogs wagging their tails when a woman offered.

"We should do this right," Liam said in a firm voice.

She shrugged. Men mystified her—they truly did. "All right. Do your worst."

"Our worst? Gaby, we're good at this," Fletch said, showing signs of an insulted male.

"You should be," she retorted. "Between the pair of you, you've been through most of Sloan's single women."

"You asked for our help." Liam rolled away from her to glower.

Yes, she had, and she was beginning to regret her request. "There's not much happening at present. You'll both deflate at this pace, undoing my good work."

"That's it," Fletch said. "Not another word or we'll gag you."

She started to reply but found her words blocked by his mouth. They emerged as unintelligible garble. Instead of taking or thrusting his tongue past her mouth and giving her an excuse to shove him off the bed, he cajoled. He licked and nibbled and sampled her mouth as if it were an expensive delicacy.

At her side, Liam started his own explorations. He brushed a trail of kisses over her shoulder and down her arm. They were delicate kisses, light as a butterfly's wing until, without warning, he changed it up. He bit the fleshy part of her arm, hard enough to jolt her. Gaby groaned into

Fletch's mouth, the shard of pain echoing in her pussy. Fletch took advantage, deepening the intimacy, tasting her with quick forays of his tongue.

Oh, these men were good.

They played her body like a musical instrument. Gaby released the last of her residual tension and let them do as they wanted. She let the pleasure rain down on her and forgot about testing her vibrator.

Liam continued to kiss his way down her arm until he reached the sensitive skin of her wrist. He pressed his lips to the base of her palm where her hand and wrist met. A shiver worked through her. The sensations grew, layering one upon another. Nothing but kisses, yet the arousal soared through her, making her pussy bloom and her breasts swell with tenderness. She wanted their mouths on her breasts. No, that wasn't right. She actively craved their touch.

Marc's casual dismissal had wounded her more than she cared to admit. But now, Fletch and Liam were soothing her pain, stoking fires inside and out. Oh yes. She couldn't wait for them to fill the empty places inside her. Their attention might be a fleeting thing, but she'd take what they offered.

A win-win situation all the way around.

Chapter Five

THE VERDICT? EVEN BETTER than he'd expected and they'd scarcely started. Fletch pulled away from kissing Gaby and absently smoothed a curl from her face as he cocked his head to learn what Liam was up to. He witnessed Liam suck one of Gaby's fingers into his mouth. Despite the innocence of the touch, Fletch's heart kicked into a crazy beat. The rhythmic hollowing of Liam's cheeks, the pause when Fletch imagined the swish of tongue translated to blatant eroticism. He imagined his cock in Liam's mouth while he caressed and teased pleasure from Gaby. Yes.

The three of them together worked perfectly, and this was just the start.

It was the sexiest thing—Liam's focus on Gaby giving Fletch the luxury of being able to stare without the need of censorship. A quick glance at Gaby reassured him. Eyelids screened her sight, her body slack with pleasure.

His two best friends. Soon his lovers. He hoped he didn't fuck up and give either of them a reason to bolt. Fletch ran a finger over Gaby's mouth, silently marveling at her softness. Liam's lips were soft too, but the contrast of stubble made their kisses different.

He turned his attention to her breasts and, unable to help himself, he wet his forefinger and drew a circle around one nipple. As he watched, it contracted, pulling tight.

"Would you like me to suck you, sweetheart?" He whispered the words, breathing warm air against the whorl of her ear at the same time. "Would you like me to suck in time with Liam?"

"Yes," she said, her reply not much more than a moan of assent.

"It will be my pleasure," he assured her.

A glance at Liam showed him his friend was watching him with a heated expression. The attention leaped straight to Fletch's dick. Hell, every naughty idea and feeling he'd suffered for the last six months fired to life with vengeance. All the cold showers and the furtive masturbating, the guilt and self-loathing for wanting the impossible had nipped at him, jeered and bashed away his inner protection.

But this once, he intended to chase what he wanted and

damn the consequences. Ten years from now he wanted to know he'd done everything he could to ensure his happiness. Even if this one day was all they had, he'd have no regrets.

Fletch winked at Liam and turned his attention to Gaby's breasts. Topped by apricot-colored nipples, they were soft and fragrant. Instead of heading straight for her nipples, he explored her shape, he tested the weight of her and licked around the base. He felt the bed move and Liam joined him. Together they explored. Their gazes caught, and although instinct suggested Fletch should stare elsewhere, he continued to watch Liam mirror his actions. He traced around Gaby's nipple, using fingers, tongue. At his side, Liam copied, his cheeks hollowing as he sucked and licked Gaby.

"Oh my stars," Gaby whispered hoarsely.

Fletch wanted to make a cheeky comment, to ask if she could see stars, but he didn't want to break the connection with Liam and he sure as hell didn't want to release her nipple. They hadn't done much yet—nothing except a little foreplay—and his cock ached for more. A good ache, the sort that foretold of mind-numbingly excellent sex.

A sharp tug on his hair made Fletch wince. His head jerked up. "Hell, woman. Don't snatch me bald."

"I need you inside me now. Now," she said in a tight

SHELLEY MUNRO

voice.

Liam let her nipple pop from his mouth. It glistened in the afternoon light. "Both of us?"

"Now," Gaby gritted out in a harsh voice, full of need.

Fletch reached for the lube. "Have you done this before?"

"Anal, yes. Two men, no."

"Maybe we should go a bit slower."

Gaby lurched up and grabbed him by the ears. She yanked his face closer. "I know my body. I want sex. I want sex *now*."

"Okay." To Fletch's relief, she released his ears and he moved out of her reach, eyeing her ruefully. He turned to Liam. "You okay with this?"

"Yes." Liam's eyes glittered. "How do you want to do this?"

Fletch wanted to shout out loud at the banked passion in Liam. It wasn't only for Gaby. Some of it was for him. He cleared his throat, testing the hard knock to his equilibrium. The lingering fears he'd experienced since the idea first occurred to him eased. This was a good start. Maybe a threesome between them wouldn't turn to shit after all. "You take the bottom."

Liam gently pushed Gaby away from the center of the bed. She whimpered in protest at the loss of contact until

80

Fletch lifted her over Liam. Liam took over, grabbing her by the hips and guiding his cock to her entrance. Gaby ceased her fighting and sank down with a groan. The entire time Liam watched Fletch, their gazes holding and feeling like a tangible contact.

"About time," she muttered.

"Did you know she was so bossy in bed?" Liam asked, humor lighting his face.

"It comes with the territory," Gaby said. "Since I chose to work at Fancy Free, I needed to lose my hang-ups about sex and ask for what I wanted. Actually, I promised myself I'd always demand what I needed after my university boyfriend dumped me. He told everyone I was crap in bed when I was merely following his lead. He didn't know his way around a woman's body and blamed the fizzer sex on me. I always regret not speaking up. Women don't have to lie there and think of England like they did fifty or a hundred years ago."

"Wow, a hot button," Liam said.

"As long as you guys both know where to find my hot button. If you're not sure of anything, ask."

Right. She'd asked for it. "I'm worried about hurting you. If you weren't in such an all-fire hurry, we could do this right and take our time."

"I told you I've designed a butt plug. I've done a lot of

research. You know the dresser in my bedroom, the kitset one you guys spent an entire day putting together?"

Fletch grimaced and saw an echoing sentiment on Liam's face. "The person who designed the dresser wasn't a builder." Sadists did the designs, and they must laugh their asses off at the mess their customers made attempting to put the bloody things together.

"We can hardly forget," Liam said, reaching up to tweak one pouting nipple. Payback.

"It's full of sex toys. Butt plugs, vibrators, nipple clamps, cock sleeves. You name it and I probably have a version. I've used all of them in my research."

"The woman has hidden talents." Fletch checked Liam's reaction. Their gazes held for a long moment. A jolt went through him, although he didn't think Liam noticed. That was the thing. Liam didn't have any idea of the way Fletch felt about him.

"Well, this woman wishes you'd stop flapping your gums and get to the action." She squirmed a little before rising and slowly sinking back down. "Ooh, that feels good."

"Enough of that," Fletch said, and he swatted her arse to reinforce the order.

She froze before glancing over her shoulder, a wicked grin twisting her lips. "Have I mentioned I like a little pain with my lovin'? I don't know why but it makes me hot."

"We'll keep that in mind," Liam said, his tone strained. "Gaby's right. You need to move things along."

Fletch opened the plain bottle and squirted a dollop of lube into his palm. Then, he gently pushed Gaby down into Liam's arms for better access. He ran his lube-free palm over Gaby's butt, a silent signal to tell her he was about to start. Bearing her impatience in mind, he didn't waste time. He slicked the lube over her pucker and carefully pushed in one finger. Gaby twisted and squirmed at the intrusion, her range of movement inhibited now that Liam filled her. Fletch pressed a hand to her back.

"Distract her for me," he said to Liam.

"Good idea. I could do with some distraction too." Without another word, Liam crushed his mouth to hers.

Immediately, Gaby ceased her writhing. Fletch gradually added another finger, taking things slowly despite her reassurance she'd take him easily. Hot flesh clamped his fingers and a frisson of excitement flooded him. Not only would he touch Gaby, he'd experience the friction of Liam's cock again. He'd been dying to repeat the experience ever since Jenny May and he trembled with eagerness. Despite that, he took time to slick his cock with lube, the warmth of his hand almost searing through the thin condom.

He sucked in a breath, deep and a little unsteady, his

mouth dry while his heart thudded with anticipation.

"Are you guys ready for this?"

Liam separated their mouths long enough to answer in the affirmative before kissing Gaby again. Easy to see Liam's increasingly urgent hunger. Fletch fastened his hands on her hips and guided his cock into position. He pushed slowly but with determination, the tight pucker creating a pressure around his cock that was almost painful. He paused, retreated a fraction before invading again. This time her sphincter muscles gave and he sank deep into her heat.

"Okay, Gaby?"

"We're fine," Liam answered.

"I can feel you both." Fletch brushed a kiss over Gaby's shoulder then leaned down to aim a kiss at Liam too. Part of him wondered if Liam might balk at another kiss. He'd pushed his luck enough already, but to his surprise, Liam's lips moved against his, the intimacy shooting an arrow of heat through him. Gasping, he pulled back, mesmerized by the hunger in Liam's eyes. "Ready to start?"

"Let's do this," Liam said.

They started to thrust in counterpoint. The cotton quilt rustled faintly each time they moved while the scent of sex and a faint trace of soap filled the air. Between them, Gaby shuddered and cried out. He pulled out and Liam pushed into Gaby. On each sweet slide, their cocks met between the thin barrier separating them. They repeated the action again and again until Fletch drifted, awash in a world of pleasure. He was vaguely aware of Gaby coming, the tight squeeze of her channel around his cock almost doing him in. Damn, this was good, even better than he'd remembered.

"How are you doing, sweetheart?"

"I'm good." She sounded satisfied and sated like a sleepy kitten.

"Liam?"

"Keep moving," his friend ordered.

Not a problem. Even though he appreciated Gaby, this time it seemed more about him and Liam. His balls lifted even as he imagined them together, freely touching and giving pleasure to each other. He pulled out of Gaby, hissing at the scrape of Liam's cock against the sensitive crown of his dick. He started to drive faster, thrusting harder until he reached the point of no return. His climax burst over him, and he could have sworn he heard bells ringing, fireworks, the entire extravaganza as pleasure dragged him under.

A rough growl vibrated through Liam, and Fletch felt a faint pulse against his cock. He squeezed his eyes closed and bit down on his tongue to halt the words waiting to spring from his mouth.

It was too early for a confession.

Despite the urgency thrumming through him, he needed to exercise patience. Only then might he have a chance to fulfill his goal of hooking up with both Liam and Gaby on a permanent basis.

Aware he was heavy and probably squashing his lovers, he carefully withdrew. He wasn't surprised when his legs wobbled. It took time for blood to return to the brain, especially after an experience as phenomenal as the one he'd just encountered.

He waited a couple of seconds, and once sure of his balance, he headed for the bathroom. Fletch removed the condom and washed up. He dampened another cloth with warm water, wrung it out and returned to the bedroom.

He found Gaby and Liam exactly where he'd left them. With a chuckle, he swatted Gaby over the butt. "Do you need help to move?"

"I'm quite comfortable where I am, thank you. I'm thinking I might go to sleep like this."

Fletch stroked the creamy skin of her bottom then used the cloth to clean her up. She sighed, widening her stance for him. With the job done, he returned the cloth to the bathroom.

Liam and Gaby were kissing when he returned to his

bedroom. A raft of emotions struck him, twisting in his chest. First the sense of rightness hit him—they were both in his bed—but swift on the heels of the initial rush of satisfaction came apprehension, a touch of envy. Then he reminded himself they were his friends and this wasn't a competition. Patience. Trust needed time to develop and cement them together.

He'd told Liam they needed to court Gaby and woo her to their way of thinking. In truth, his mission was twofold because he was desperate to convince Liam of the magical possibilities in their future. A wooing within a wooing.

The woo-woo factor.

Chapter Six

LIAM WRAPPED HIS ARMS around Gaby and continued with the lazy kissing. Long, sensuous kisses. Gentle suction as their tongues swirled together in a silent dance of desire. Quick nibbling kisses that made the blood roar through his veins, made his cock pulse with renewed longing.

A hungry sound escaped her and his emotions rocked in victory. Physical attraction was half the battle, and they already had the friendship to bolster the blooming magnetism between them.

"You two going to keep up with that all afternoon or are we going to test some sex toys?" A faint snap cloaked Fletch's words and Liam smirked against Gaby's lips.

She lifted her head and grinned over her shoulder. "Just keeping warmed up."

"You wanted us to work out the toys ourselves?" Fletch asked.

"Yes. I want to make sure my instructions are clear."

Liam watched Fletch closely. Normally he could tell Fletch's mood with a quick glance. Not today. His friend had instigated two kisses with him, and he wasn't sure how to feel or what to think about the physical contact with a man he called friend. He should probably punch Fletch's lights out and go from there, yet he couldn't seem to build up a good head of indignation. He found himself scowling in the direction of Fletch's mouth and ripped his gaze away. Confusion didn't begin to cover the emotions blindsiding him today.

At a crossroads, he didn't know which way to turn. A part of him wanted to sprint back down the road he'd already traveled, while his adventurous soul pushed him to stride bravely forward, following the route he and Fletch discussed the previous day.

"Here," Fletch said, snaring Liam's full attention.

Gaby lifted away from him, separating their bodies.

Liam dealt with the condom before accepting the vibrator. He studied the toy, smoothing his fingers over the penis-shaped attachment. "Looks simple enough." He hit the power button. Instantly a low drone filled the room and the attachment started moving forward and back in a thrusting motion.

Fletch grinned. "At a guess, I'd say that bit is the

substitute penis and goes in the vagina or tickles the clit."

"Good." Gaby clapped her hands together, a beam of satisfaction on her face. She never confided details of her work—a confidentiality clause, so she said—and Liam found this glimpse fascinating.

"Can we try it?" Fletch plucked the vibe from Liam and switched the power off. "What do the other attachments do?" He reached over to grab the bag of attachments.

Liam followed the move, his gaze fixing on Fletch's arse. When the urge to touch struck out of the blue, a croak of shock burst from him. He ripped his gaze away, his heartbeat galloping in echo of his shock. He was ogling his best friend's backside.

Fletch turned back to them and, unbidden, Liam's attention fixed on his friend again. Their eyes met. Hell. Liam wanted to look away yet, contrarily, he craved the intimate connection with Fletch. His friend didn't seem to hold the same scruples or doubts. He stared right back, comfortable in his own skin. His lips curled upward and he winked.

"I vote we go for this attachment." Fletch held up one with a little roller.

"One of my personal favorites," Gaby said. "I got the inspiration from the massage chairs at the mall. This roller bit stimulates either side of the clit. There's another bottle of lube. Can you pass that to me?"

Liam climbed off the bed to do her bidding. "What's so special about this lube?"

"Ah, just wait and see," she said with a teasing smile.

"Did you realize your music player was in here?" Fletch asked, still poring through the bag.

Gaby nodded. "Yep." She commandeered the lube from him and opened the bottle. She squirted some onto her palm and turned to Fletch. "You first. Lie back and close your eyes."

After Fletch closed his eyes, Liam felt able to study him openly, visually examining the lines of his body, his muscular build and finally, his cock. Gaby teased Fletch, running her fingers up and down his length and, as he watched, Fletch grew erect. Then she applied the lube with languid strokes. Fletch kept his eyes shut, but Liam had no trouble seeing how Fletch felt about Gaby's hand massage. His cock lengthened under her ministrations, his balls drawing up rapidly. His heartfelt moan of pleasure sealed the deal as did the musky scent of arousal filling the bedroom.

"Hand me the vibe please."

Liam handed her the vibrator and soon the low motorized hum sounded. Gaby used the attachment to add additional stimulation. She ran it over his balls and

SHELLEY MUNRO

lower to vibrate along his perineum.

Until today Liam had never studied another man so intimately. It wasn't the done thing to ogle another man's junk in the showers after rugby training but, right now, he couldn't have shifted his gaze if he wanted to. Part of him wanted to participate, to lean lower and lick the bead of pre-come from the slit of Fletch's cock. He shifted uncomfortably, aware of the echoing arousal in his own body.

He wanted to experience Fletch, in exactly the same way as Gaby. Swift on the heels of the thought came fear.

Panic.

God, he'd be the butt of everyone's jokes if they ever learned his thoughts. It was bad enough with his mother and the way she soaked up booze and drugs and jumped into bed with every man who took her fancy. A shudder worked down to his gut. Thank god, she hadn't returned to Sloan for several months. His life was more peaceful when his mother stayed away.

"Describe the sensations to me," Gaby said with a final leisurely stroke, dragging Liam's thoughts back to the present. "Do you like them or are they too intense?"

"They feel great now, but I think if you used the vibrator on me for much longer, the sensation would become painful."

"Liam, I want your opinion. Lie beside Fletch. Fletch I'm going to stroke for a bit longer. Tell me when the friction becomes too much for you."

Liam settled beside Fletch, his pulse skittering at the blast of heat coming off his friend. Already his imagination was doing things to his cock and Gaby hadn't started.

"Enough," Fletch said, his eyes popping open. "I'll come if you do that for much longer."

"Okay." She stopped instantly and turned away to jot a note on her clipboard. "What do you think of the lube?"

"It sort of heats yet chills at the same time. It's hard to describe."

"Too much? Did the vibrator contribute to that? Or was it solely the lube?" Gaby fired questions like a drillmaster. "What's your normal recovery power like?"

Liam listened to Fletch's honest answers, fascinated despite himself. When men discussed sex, it was more about the scoring. They never discussed details like this.

"Your turn now." Gaby squirted another dollop of lube on her palm and grinned at Liam. "Ready?"

"Go on. Do your worst." Fletch rolled over to his side, bringing him closer to Liam. "He can take the torture."

Desire jolted Liam, and his lids fell to half-mast in an attempt to screen his reaction. Did Fletch realize the power he held over him? Maybe he did because he seemed intent on taunting Liam and pushing him past the point of comfort. Normally, Liam wouldn't have worried. They'd challenged each other since childhood, but this was sexual in character. The possible consequences scared the shit out of him.

"Don't listen to him," Gaby said. "This time I want you to describe the sensations you feel when I apply the lube. If my touch becomes painful or uncomfortable, let me know." As she spoke, she laid her hands on him. Icy tingles shot from the point of contact, so cold his breath caught. Liam lifted up on his elbows and watched the mesmerizing stroke of Gaby's hand. Up and down. Up and down.

Gradually the cold tingles transformed. "The lube started off cold. So icy-cold it was a shock. It was like the jolt of a snowball down my back."

"And now?" Fletch asked.

Liam stilled, his attention shooting to Fletch. He forced himself not to look away. A flash of heat filled Fletch's eyes and he didn't even try to hide it. *Fuck me.* This weird shit between them wasn't his imagination.

"Liam?" Gaby's determined voice broke the spell between the two men. "How does that feel?"

Liam swallowed, heat suffusing his cheeks when Fletch winked at him. "Your hand has heated the lube. The tingling is sharper. It hasn't faded even with the heat of your hand. I'm not sure if it's the lube or you, but I'm not gonna be able to hold back much longer."

"Does it hurt?" Fletch whispered next to his ear.

The puff of warm air zapped straight to his shaft. Aw, hell.

"Fletch, this should work on nipples too. Liam, is it okay if Fletch applies some to your nipples. You won't get funny about him touching you?"

Hell, no matter what he said he was screwed. Either he disappointed Gaby or he let Fletch touch him and add layers of experiences, memories to an imagination that didn't need help thank you very much.

"Liam, you gonna let me touch you?" The siren whisper next to his ear sent another jolt straight to his cock.

"Bastard," Liam muttered.

"Say the words, Liam. I want your permission."

Gaby applied more lube and swished her hand up and down his shaft. The initial chill pulled him back from the wall, giving him a semblance of control.

"Go ahead," he said, tension killing some of his eagerness.

"Comments?" Gaby demanded.

She was kinda cute in her bossy inventor role. "When you added more lube, the chill helped me step back a bit. I don't feel as if I'm going to come any second now."

Gaby released his cock for an instant to jot a note. The absence of heat from her hand caused another different sensation—a prickling awareness. Anticipation of good things to come.

"I'm going to use my mouth on you soon to test the taste of the lube and I want you to describe how my touch feels. Fletch, you go first. Spread a little lube with your fingers. Give Liam a chance to catalog the sensations and describe them to me. Then I want you to use your mouth." She must have caught the trace of panic in his expression because she paused. "Will you mind Fletch touching you? Do you want me to do it?"

"You worried people are gonna think you're gay?" Fletch drawled.

"Don't be stupid! No one thinks you're gay," Gaby said. "Women have been chasing you since you turned sixteen."

"Rachel Scott watches you every time you're in the same room," Fletch added with a faint smirk.

"You could do worse," Gaby agreed. "Helping me test my inventions won't get in the way of your relationship, will it?"

"I'm not interested in Rachel." To his intense shame, he'd drunk a little much one night two weeks ago and succumbed. They'd slept together and he'd spent the whole night imagining he was fucking Gaby. He'd been ducking Rachel ever since, embarrassed by his behavior. Not his finest moment. Probably time to man up and talk to Rachel, let her down gently.

"Does she know that?" his friend asked.

Liam glared at Fletch. "I've been busy lately."

Fletch sent him a mocking grin before squirting lube into the palm of his hand. Liam's breath caught. He watched Fletch dip a forefinger in the lube.

"You ready?" he murmured for Liam's hearing only.

"Bring it." Fighting words.

Fletch merely grinned and skimmed his finger around one of Liam's nipples. A chill swept him, much like the one when Gaby applied the lube to his cock. Gradually, Fletch changed the pressure and the way he stroked Liam's nipple. He swapped between firm and whisper soft. Pleasure darted through Liam, firing erogenous zones to life all over his body. Women had played with his nipples before and he'd never experienced much sensation. Maybe it was the lube, but each touch seemed sharper and did interesting things to his libido.

He hesitated, trying to put his responses into words for Gaby. He didn't want to give Fletch the wrong idea. His throat worked in a swallow before he could formulate the words. *Go on, get it out, man.* "The lube seems to intensify sensations. There was the same initial shock of ice when

Fletch applied it."

"And now?"

Yeah, she was gonna make him tell her everything. Liam sucked in a deep breath. "Every time he touches my nipple, it feels as if there's a direct pathway to my cock. You're not touching me now. Only Fletch. That should make me soften. Instead I feel as if I could hammer nails with my dick." There. He'd confessed. Fletch touching him didn't turn him off. He obviously wasn't a normal male.

"Good. Perfect. That's the response I was looking for. I had the same reaction when I tested the lube on my nipples."

Fletch's head lifted. Mischief sparkled in him, and Liam guessed the words zapping through his friend's mind. "You have a cock? It must be a retractable one because I can't see a dickie bird."

"You're an ass sometimes, Fletch." Gaby flashed her pussy in their direction. "See anything retractable?"

"No, sweetheart," Fletch said.

"Now you know." She wrapped Ms. Inventor mode around her again and tapped her pen on the clipboard. "Use your mouth. Tell me how you like the taste. Tell me if the lube causes any irritation."

"Yes ma'am." A verbal salute.

Liam braced himself for the heat of Fletch's mouth. His

hands clenched at his sides. Fletch spread on a little more lube, painting some on each nipple this time. Before he could fully categorize the sensations, Fletch lowered his head and sucked hard on one nipple. Pleasure streaked down his body. Sharp like a spear, it cut straight to his cock. His hips jerked. A moan squeezed past his lips, and before he knew it, his hands were in Fletch's hair and he was holding Fletch too him, his cock stabbing into empty air.

"Jeez, Fletch. Stop," he croaked as climax started to roar through him.

"You'll have to let me go first."

A flush swept over his face. He had to force his fingers to unlock and release his friend.

"Why did you stop?" Gaby demanded.

"I didn't think Fletch would appreciate me coming all over him," Liam said hoarsely. His pulse was still thundering as if he were running a race.

The stiff tension left Gaby and she grinned. "Good. That's good. The lube made me super hot but I wasn't sure if it was a one-off." As she spoke, she reached for a condom and rolled it on his cock. "We still need to test the sex toys but this should help ease some of your tension." She impaled herself and rose leisurely up and down.

Liam relaxed a fraction, sinking into the mattress and

letting the sensations roll over him.

Fletch leaned close and whispered in his ear. "Do you want me to touch you?"

A curl of heat writhed through his groin, hunger consuming him like a rogue wave. His nipples drew painfully tight on hearing the husky note in Fletch's voice. "Yeah." His voice merged hoarse, a touch uncertain, but his friend never hesitated.

Fletch painted his nipple with more lube in a deliberate manner. Heat flowed from his nipple, switching to ferocious the instant Fletch applied his mouth. Oh hell. His hips snapped upward, the hot, tight suction driving him past the point of no return. He exploded into climax, unable to hold back an instant longer. Liam shoved Fletch away from him, the contact too much. His chest rose and fell as he dragged in huge drafts of air. "Sorry," he said. "I could *not* hold back."

"Simultaneous climax is not expected, especially when we're testing products. Besides, I can demonstrate an attachment now." She separated their bodies and turned to reach for her clipboard. After jotting a few notes, she leaned over and picked up the vibrator. She exchanged attachments, clicking one with a set of rollers and a curving part.

"What does that bit do?" Liam asked, fascinated despite

the lethargy from orgasm.

"Wait and see." She stretched out beside Liam and parted her legs without the slightest hint of awkwardness.

"So pretty," Fletch said. "Can I touch?"

"I would like to test the lube on my nipples."

Fletch saluted, a cheeky grin in place. "Certainly, my lady." He reached for the lube and squeezed a dollop on his palm. He lifted a brow in Liam's direction. "Gaby has two beautiful breasts."

Liam finally stirred and pushed to a sitting position. He dipped a finger in the lube on Fletch's hand and turned back to Gaby. A drone filled the bedroom when she switched on the vibrator. Liam watched her insert the vibrator into her pussy and position the roller attachment to revolve on either side of her clit rather than giving direct stimulation.

"That bit stimulates the G-spot. Right?" Curiosity propelled him to ask questions. "Does one size fit all? What about the women who don't know their bodies?"

"Find me one," Gaby said instantly, raising her voice over the buzz of the vibrator. She angled it slightly, a shudder going through her. A faint flush colored her cheeks. Beautiful. Just beautiful. "I'd like to talk to someone who doesn't know what they're doing. Most teenagers learn about sex early these days. They're more aware of their bodies. Ooh, damn that feels good."

"Ready?" Fletch asked.

"Yes," Gaby wailed, her back arching upward.

Liam chuckled, totally understanding the need coursing through her. "I think he was talking to me."

"Stop talking," Gaby ordered. "Apply the lube."

After a quick glance at him, Fletch applied the lube to Gaby's nipple and Liam followed suit. Together, they licked and sucked. The buzz of the vibrator became louder and Gaby let out a whimper, her hips gyrating. A body shudder swept through her. Liam lifted his head and watched the fog of desire take her. She was gorgeous in her surrender, her cheeks flushed and her head thrown back.

He grinned at Fletch and his friend tossed back a smile. Job well done.

Chapter Seven

Gaby met them at the door a few days later. "Hey, I thought you'd never get home."

"You look beautiful," Liam said, and it was nothing less than the truth. She'd done something with cosmetics to make her eyes mysterious and smoky. They were used to seeing her in jeans and T-shirts. Today she wore a figure-skimming dress that hit a touch above her knees.

Liam's heart sank, and he sent a swift glance at Fletch. His best friend didn't seem any happier than him. Despite the intimacies and the fun they'd had testing Gaby's inventions. The pretty sunset-colored dress told the story, one he didn't like a single bit.

"Do you have a date?" Fletch opened the fridge and pulled out two cans of beer, handing one to him.

"I'm going to dinner at my parents' place. It's my nephew's birthday." Gaby wrinkled her nose. "It's a command performance. I try not to give my mother anything to complain about. No doubt she'll find something."

Relief struck Liam in a heady rush.

"You look great," Fletch said, some of the tension leaving his shoulders. "Are you wearing panties?"

Liam barked out a laugh as Gaby's brows shot upward.

"I'm visiting my parents," she said, disbelief coloring her tone.

"Work with me here," Fletch said. "Are they at least sexy ones?"

Liam chuckled at the glint in his friend's eyes. "He wants to take a peek."

Gaby backed up, holding her hand in front of her in a silent stop sign. "You've just come off a building site."

Fletch sent her a wicked grin and advanced half a step.

"I have to go or I'll be late," she said in a breathless rush. "I've left a package of toys for you guys to test for me. They're on Fletch's bed." Gaby seized her handbag, her bunch of car keys and fled.

Liam took a sip of his beer, his gut bucking at the idea of testing more toys. Why had Gaby mentioned the toys now instead of waiting until she'd returned home? So far, they'd spent the last three nights in Fletch's bed, testing toys together. He slid a glance in Fletch's direction and caught him staring. "What?"

"I was wondering why Gaby mentioned the toys now rather than later."

"Me too."

"Gaby slept with us the entire night again instead of returning to her bedroom like she did after testing the first lot of toys."

"Do you think that means anything?"

"Hard to say." Fletch paused, frowned. "You've stayed every night since we started this."

A swirl of heat started in the base of his gut and swelled until it reached his cheeks. He slurped his beer in an attempt at nonchalance. Yeah, it was true, and Liam wasn't certain what to make of his willingness to get close and personal with another male. The day before yesterday he'd woken wrapped around Fletch. His friend hadn't stirred, and he'd moved away before things became even stranger between them.

So far, the weirdness hadn't affected their working relationship.

Liam swallowed the last of his beer before setting the can on the counter. "I'm gonna have a shower."

"Coward."

"Who are you calling a coward?"

"Don't you want to check out the package Gaby left for

us?"

"It's in your room." Liam turned before Fletch came up with something else to embarrass him. He was fine at work but once they reached home, he didn't play by the rules. Liam didn't know what to think. Hell, he tried not to think about Fletch because for some weird reason he'd started getting a hard-on.

Liam stalked from the kitchen without looking back. The weight of Fletch's stare followed him until he reached the passage, making him edgy. Restless. *Hell*.

In the bathroom, he stripped off his clothes, leaving them in a heap on the floor. He flipped on the taps, setting both showerheads going. After stepping under the water, he absently grabbed the soap to lather his chest.

He wouldn't put it past Fletch to burst in on him. His friend went out of his way to touch him when they were alone. If he told Fletch to fuck off and knock off the touchy-feely shit, he'd probably obey without comment. Part of him wanted Fletch to back off, yet the other part—he cast a disgruntled glare at his erection—wanted to follow the possibilities and damn other people's perceptions.

Gaby and Fletch had led him astray.

Liam barked out a sudden laugh. He hadn't exactly fought them, merely followed like a docile lamb.

FLETCH HEARD THE SHOWER start, but not a shred of the tension left his shoulders. The ring of a cell phone snared his attention. Liam's. He glanced at the screen and replaced it on the counter, his mind drifting back to Gaby and Liam. Something on Gaby's face made him suspect the toys she'd left for them would push them farther than they'd traveled to date.

With his beer in hand, he wandered down the passage toward his bedroom. His steps slowed as he passed the bathroom. He forced himself to keep moving when what he wanted was to push open the door and step into the shower with Liam. His cock pressed against his fly, echoing approval of his thoughts. Despite his constant hard-on, he'd managed to keep his seduction subtle enough to escape the notice of others. During work hours, he'd kept things strictly businesslike. He didn't want to scare Liam off before he'd hooked and reeled him in.

In his bedroom, he stripped to his boxer-briefs before sitting on the bed to investigate the contents of the bag Gaby had left for them.

Well hell.

Butt plugs in several designs. One looked as if it might

vibrate while another was the standard type—not that he'd had much experience with plugs. One of his past girlfriends had liked using them, saying she experienced fantastic orgasms with a plug stuffed in her rear passage. There were a couple of smaller ones that didn't look so scary, along with more bottles of lube. Gaby was big on her lube.

"Butt plugs?"

Fletch's head jerked up to see Liam standing in the doorway, a towel wrapped around his waist. "Yeah. You ever used one?"

"Once," Liam said with a cautious glance at him.

"Yeah? How did it feel?"

"It hurt a bit at first."

Fletch frowned. "And after?"

"I had a great weekend," Liam said. "Have any of your lovers stroked your prostrate while sucking you off?"

"Yeah, a couple." Fletch stared at his friend, uncertain of what to say, how to proceed. Gaby's presence made it easy for him to touch Liam. She made their intimacies seem natural. Now alone with his friend, indecision tied his gut in knots. "Hey, your cell phone rang while you were in the shower."

"Who was it?"

"Rachel. I didn't answer, just glanced at the screen."

"I'll ring her later."

"You still going out with her?"

"No. We went out twice. I haven't asked her out again. No chemistry."

"Ouch. Did you tell her?"

"No. I don't want to talk about Rachel." Liam stepped into his bedroom, and Fletch's pulse did a quick two-step before resuming its regular pace. "You normally have a lot more to say."

"I don't want to spoil our friendship. It means a lot to me," Fletch said.

A snort emerged from Liam as he stepped closer to the bed without taking his gaze off Fletch. "Having second thoughts about touching me?"

The undercurrents swirling between them took a sharp dive into a different beast. *Tread carefully*. "I don't want to mess things up between us."

"Your scruples didn't stop you kissing me, taking liberties." Liam came to a stop in front of him. "I can't believe you're having doubts now. You never second-guess yourself."

"Always a first time," Fletch muttered, unable to meet Liam's gaze for an instant longer. His gaze shot to the cock-shaped plug he held in one hand. *Shit, not helping*. His mind careered out of control, sending blood pooling to his groin.

"Yeah, well here's the thing," Liam said. "Since we started having sex with Gaby, I haven't been able to think of much else. I'm having trouble concentrating at work. Your fault, Fletch. It's not just Gaby but you too. I find myself wanting to touch you at the most inappropriate moments. When I kiss Gaby goodbye, I want to do the same to you." Liam glared at him as if he were to blame.

Fletch opened his mouth and closed it again without uttering a word. Hell, maybe the sexual tension between them was his fault. He'd started them on this journey.

"Now Gaby is in on the act, producing butt plugs for us to test."

"We could do our testing alone," Fletch protested, feeling as if the conversation was rolling away without him, like one of those runaway trains in the movies. Liam didn't normally say this much unless he felt strongly on a subject.

Liam cocked his head, a sexy grin breaking past the pissed attitude. "Now where would be the fun in that?"

Fletch stared at his friend, still speechless. Liam's childhood had left him shy and he still tended to keep to the background unless the situation was work related or if he knew the person well. He certainly never lacked for feminine company, which was why Fletch had hesitated to approach him.

"Nothing to say?" Liam taunted.

"Fuck no. I've got plenty to say. I'm trying to decide if I should."

Liam's brows shot upward toward his hairline. "You've never hesitated before."

"I've never had this much at stake before," Fletch shot back before his brain censored him.

Liam fell silent and actually took half a step back.

Fletch's hand clenched around the plug. *Hellshitfuckdamn.* Now he'd done it. If he hadn't scared Liam off before, he would now with his declaration of intent. He wasn't chasing Liam for fun and giggles.

Liam's chest rose and fell, attracting Fletch's attention. A couple of droplets of water glinted on his skin, and the urge to stand and lick them away shot through Fletch. He gripped the plug even harder and forced himself to look away.

"Good to hear. I wouldn't want to think you were messing with me."

The weird note in Liam's voice dragged his gaze right back, and when Fletch met his gaze, Liam dropped the towel from around his waist.

He had an erection.

As Fletch stared, Liam's erection grew.

Liam coughed, diverting his attention. "Yeah. I have a

thing for you too. Why don't you go and have a shower?"

Fletch swallowed to dislodge the lump in his throat. Not in a million years had he seen their conversation going this way. "What are you going to do?"

Liam sent him a crooked grin, his hand going down to stroke his cock. Fletch followed the motion with his gaze and felt an answering surge in his own dick.

"I'm going to be a good soldier and test one of the plugs for Gaby. Don't take long in the shower because I might need some help."

Elation surged through Fletch at Liam's words. Part of him was shit-scared at the rapid shift in their friendship, but he couldn't say he didn't want this. It was the stuff of dreams. His dreams. "Are you sure?"

"No, but I don't like confusion. I'd rather know."

Yeah, made sense. Fletch gave a curt nod and hurried from the bedroom before he did something stupid like grabbing his best friend and laying a hard kiss on his sexy lips.

Liam stared after Fletch, aware of a blip of excitement in his gut despite his misgivings. He stepped over the fallen towel. Fletch had left the plugs sitting on the bed. He picked the closest one up and tested the weight. It looked like the one he'd tried—a classic cone shape. Made of a glasslike material, the plug was red and white. When he pressed a small button at the end of the flared base, the plug flashed like a candy cane. A snigger broke out. The candy-cane effect would be lost while the plug was in use. He picked up the other one. Vibrating. He pushed another button on the base and the tinny sound of a familiar Christmas carol filled the room. A smirk formed this time and he didn't think he'd ever listen to the lyrics about snow and dashing without imagining sex.

His investigation of the bag produced two smaller probe plugs, perfect for use for beginners, along with more lube.

Fletch arrived in the bedroom and didn't halt his approach until he reached the bed.

"Quick shower."

"I didn't want you to change your mind."

Fletch's honesty reassured Liam. While part of his mind shouted he was making a mistake, the rest of him settled in edgy anticipation. If he didn't pursue this between them, he'd regret the lost opportunity. He refused to turn and walk away now. He'd always wonder if he followed that path.

"How do you want to do this?" Now they came to the realities, his bravado started to falter. Scared didn't begin to cover his feelings right this minute.

"I haven't thought much beyond the wanting," Fletch

admitted.

Liam's throat worked, the weight of Fletch's attention sending his nerves swirling through his gut. The beer he'd drunk earlier churned. Hell, maybe they were both guilty of over-thinking this situation.

"Join me on the bed," he said finally. "What do you do when you're with a new woman?"

"Simple," Fletch said. "Some light petting and lots of kissing until she relaxes. The more foreplay the better the lay."

"You don't say." Liam couldn't help his dry tone. Fletch's casual approach to women cracked him up. Another thought occurred and jealousy ratcheted upward in him. "You better not be pulling your spread-'em-around shit with me."

"I want Gaby, and as far as I'm concerned, you're part of the package. I want you too." Fletch crawled onto the bed and smoothly rolled against him. He never hesitated as he leaned over Liam and started kissing.

A rush of pleasure settled on Liam when their lips met. There was none of the tentativeness of their earlier kisses. They angled their heads, mouths moving together naturally. Their tongues touched as they explored each other. He tasted beer and Fletch. His arms wrapped around his friend and he tried to get closer. Their chests rubbed together. The faint tickle of chest hair threw him for a moment—Fletch had chest hair while he didn't have much. Firm muscles met his and the differences didn't scare him.

He parted their mouths to stare at Fletch. "I'm a breast man."

Fletch spluttered a laugh. "You won't find any here."

"That's not what I meant. I like kissing you and it surprised me."

"But would you like to kiss another guy?"

"No! No, of course not." His answer came quickly, so readily he knew it was the truth. While a part of him might have feared an outbreak of gayness, that didn't appear the case. Fletch did it for him. Fletch and Gaby. Together or separately.

"So you're not frightened of my erection?" Fletch gestured at his cock with a sly grin.

"Are you trying to scare me off?"

"No, I'm trying to settle my nerves with humor."

Silence fell. They stared at each other and burst into laughter, falling against each other until their hilarity faded.

"We're really gonna do this?" Liam asked.

"Yeah. At least, I want to."

"Good." And he dived in to kiss Fletch again, using his

hands this time, feeling free to explore the muscles and body he'd recently started fantasizing about. When their groins touched, their cocks brushing, he didn't freeze up. He closed his eyes and went with the physical sensations racing through him. A little naughtiness. Definitely desire, the urge to do more.

"Can I touch you?"

Liam didn't even open his eyes. "Please."

One word taking them even farther onto the path of what most people considered wrong. Funny how it felt so right.

Fletch slid his body closer and reached down to grasp his cock. Liam gasped. With his sight screened, he could almost imagine it was his own hand curled around his shaft. But it was Fletch's musky scent and the faint citrus from the body wash he'd used that grounded Liam. Fletch's big hand added his own cock to the mix and started moving slowly. A jolt went through Liam. He swallowed, let a moan loose.

"Feels damn good, doesn't it?"

"Yeah." An understatement.

Fletch's hand went up and down, gradually increasing in speed. His touch wasn't tentative or gentle. Instinctively he did exactly what Liam liked to do whenever he wanted to get himself off. Needing more, Liam turned his head and blindly sought Fletch's mouth. He inhaled and kissed his friend, using his tongue like a cock. Invading, pushing them both into quick arousal, hot pleasure. Liam's balls started to draw up and he couldn't summon a single bit of shame, not when he felt so good.

He wanted this, wanted more.

The uneven thumping of his heart turned even more erratic, and suddenly he couldn't hold back the pleasure. He toppled over into a furious climax, shooting cum in hard bursts. Fletch came a few seconds later and eased off on the hand action. Their mouths parted and they stared at each other, uncomfortable in the aftermath of such unrestrained pleasure.

"Are you gonna freak now?" Fletch asked, his voice toneless.

"Nope."

"What? That's it?"

"We could discuss this to death or we could move on and take each day as it happens." Hell, he'd already thought things to death. They didn't need to talk as well. "I'll grab a cloth to clean us up." He rolled away from Fletch and prowled down the passage to the bathroom. On automatic pilot, he grabbed a cloth and waited for the water to run hot. He cleaned himself off, refreshed the cloth and returned to Fletch's bedroom.

He found Fletch staring at the butt plugs, a perplexed expression on his face. In his other hand, he held Gaby's list of instructions. "Tell me you can work this stuff. I know the mechanics but..." He trailed off, grimacing at Liam.

"You still haven't worked up the courage to try it, huh?"

"No."

"Do you trust me?"

Fletch lost some of the color from his face but nodded.

Liam couldn't believe he intended to do this, although they'd gone way past friendship already. He grabbed the instruction sheet from Fletch, scanned them and picked up one of the thinner probe plugs plus a bottle of lube. "Lie on your back, spread your legs. I'll add lube first and stretch you a little first to get you used to my touch. Once you're comfortable, I'll put in the plug. Okay?"

Big, super-confident Fletch swallowed, appearing distinctly nervous. "All right."

"Relax."

"Easy for you to say."

"How about I put one in me first?"

"Good idea," Fletch said, relief shading his voice.

Liam grabbed one of the thinner butt plugs plus the lube. Green in color, it was flexible and had a flared base like the others. It had a button on the base, and when he pushed it, the entire thing flashed green and vibrated.

"Whoa," Fletch said.

Chuckling, Liam squirted lube onto his hand and relaxed on the mattress beside Fletch. Spreading his legs, he stroked his cock a couple of times, enough to get an erection going. Gradually, he moved lower, smoothing the lube across his pucker. Blood filled his cock rapidly, Fletch's close attention propelling his arousal as much as anything. His finger slipped past the ring of muscles, the glide of his digit moving down until it skimmed his prostate. He sighed at the rush of pleasure. Gradually he stretched his hole. Part of him wanted to close his eyes and shut out the fact he was with Fletch. Yet something in Fletch's expression, the avid way he watched made Liam so hot he wanted to burst. And the excitement wasn't just about his cock. That was the scary thing.

When his breathing turned ragged, he withdrew his fingers, lubed up the plug and inserted it carefully. Finally with the plug in place, he turned to Fletch. "You ready?"

"Let's do this."

Liam shifted, rolling up to a sitting position. He felt every shift and flex of the plug in his arse when he moved. His breath caught when the plug pressed against his prostate, acute sparks of pressure firing through his cock. He hissed and stilled.

"Problem?"

Liam laughed, the rough and husky merriment suggestive in the almost silent room. "The plug rolled against my prostate. Feels good. When I turn on the vibrator attachment, things should get interesting." He grabbed the other plug and the lube, moving between Fletch's legs. With a trembling hand, he reached for Fletch's cock. A faint edginess shimmered between them, but he batted the trepidation away. Fletch would tell him if he went too far. Besides, he'd asked for this.

Fletch focused on Liam's face. He wasn't sure about the plug, but he wanted Liam's touch so bad he'd do almost anything to get his friend's hands running over his body.

The first firm grip of his dick made his entire body hum. Liam's rough palm against his cock fueled the erotic promise in the air. The muscles of his abdomen rippled and his breath caught as he attempted to relax. The sensation of lube against his hole did nothing to cool his ardor.

Liam took things slowly, stroking his cock then probing his hole to give him maximum pleasure. The care and consideration relaxed him even more than the sharp bursts of excitement striking his cock and balls.

"Holy crap," he whispered. "I never realized this would feel so good."

"It can get even better." Liam's sly smile held promise and naughtiness. He removed his finger, leaving Fletch empty, definitely needy.

Liam lubed up the plug and pushed it against his hole. His channel rippled, almost embracing the intrusion, and Fletch arched his hips, silently asking for more. There was a slight discomfort but nothing near the pain he'd envisaged.

"All done." Liam tapped the base of the plug and he felt his channel flex around it. At the same time an electrical zap to his groin almost short-circuited his brain.

"Fuck," Fletch muttered when he could breathe again.

"You ready for a bit more?"

Fletch had no idea what Liam had in mind, but he trusted him. Just one glance at his friend sent a decadent wash of warmth through him. He stared at Liam, allowing himself to appreciate the stark, masculine beauty for the first time. "Do it." He gestured with his hands and let a grin stretch across his face. Oh yeah. He was ready for the next step.

"Okay," Liam said, and he lowered his head and took Fletch's cock into his mouth, tongue swirling while his hands massaged Fletch's balls. He tapped the base of the plug and it started to vibrate, almost sending Fletch over the edge.

"Holy hell." Breathless, he attempted to list the

sensations for Gaby's form. The plug vibrated in his channel, catching his gland now and then while heat surrounded his cock along with hard suction and unrelenting stimulation.

This was the blowjob he'd always wanted from his girlfriends. Some of them had been skilled, but not one of them anticipated his needs like Liam. Fletch focused on the pull of Liam's mouth, the stroke of his fingers and the brush of the plug against his channel. Liam's tongue fluttered over his sweet spot, and he shuddered. Unbidden, his hips lifted, driving his cock deeper into Liam's mouth. The rasp of tongue, the twist of balls brought a moan.

Somehow, Liam was keeping him on edge. Whenever he thought he'd soar into climax, Liam twisted his balls, keeping the pleasure at a low simmer.

Liam paused to lift his head. "Okay?"

"You're good at this. Anyone would think you have experience." Shit, he hadn't meant to insert the attitude, the edge of accusation.

Liam's open expression clouded over. "I haven't. I figured if I like something, you would too."

"Sorry."

Liam gave a curt nod and Fletch released his concerns. He should've known his friend wouldn't take his words the wrong way. Considering his shitty upbringing, Liam was the most even-tempered man, make that person, he'd ever met.

"Hey, enough of the talk. Get me off. Please?" Yeah, he wasn't above begging.

With another grin, Liam lowered his head again and applied suction. At the same time, he carefully twisted the plug, and it was all over Rover. Fletch couldn't have held back if he'd wanted to. The tight wire gripping his cock snapped and pleasure roared from his balls and up his cock. If he'd been thinking more clearly, he would've checked with Liam about coming inside his mouth. Too late now.

Liam continued to stroke him but eased the attention down a notch or two, swallowing around his length like a champ. Gradually Fletch returned to his body, his hoarse breathing leveling out to something approaching normal.

Liam eased back and impassive settled on his sexy face. Did he think Fletch intended to punch him? Not. Gonna. Happen.

The sex he'd experienced with both Gaby and Liam during the last week was the best of his life and he wasn't about to do anything to mess it up. Perhaps it was time to spell this out to Liam again so he didn't look like a cautious dog, expecting a whipping from its master.

"That was fuckin' awesome." He levered up and reached for Liam, planting a quick, hard kiss on his lips. "Let me catch my breath and I'll do you. I have some tricks that will make your eyes cross. How do I stop this thing vibrating?"

"There's a button in the base." Liam reached over to grab the clipboard and scribbled several notes about the plugs. "I'm writing *Easy to insert. Comfortable. Fletch loved the vibrations.* Anything else to add?"

"No, I don't think so. How long can we leave these in?"

Liam consulted Gaby's notes. "According to Gaby, they can be comfortably worn for several hours. She mentions lube for ease of use."

"Make sense." Fletch grabbed the clipboard off Liam and tossed it out of the way. "My turn now. Let's have some fun."

Chapter Eight

"How is work?" her father asked.

"Great. We're working on designs for the Christmas market," Gaby said with a quick glance at her mother.

"Do we have to talk about S E X at the dinner table?" Elsa, her sister asked. "There are children present."

"Are you making toys for Christmas?" Olivia her niece piped up.

"Yes, she is," Gaby's grandmother said. For once she'd left her knitting in its bag. No doubt the knitting needles would start flashing once they settled down to open the presents. Gaby couldn't remember a time during her childhood when her grandmother didn't have her knitting to hand, the click of needles a constant background song.

"Grownup toys," Jason Montgomery said, winking at Gaby.

"That's right," Gaby said, smiling back at her father.

"How is kindy, William? Do you like going?"

"Yes." Her nephew beamed at her, his face glowing with excitement. In under an hour his friends would start to arrive to help him celebrate his birthday. "Mama packs my lunch every day and we learn to write our names and numbers. Lots of things," he said, scarcely pausing to take breath.

Both her niece and nephew adored kindy. While she and Elsa might disagree about a lot of things, Elsa was a brilliant mother and wife.

Gaby nodded. "Where's Allan? Is he working?"

"He's wiring a house for Liam and Fletch," Elsa said. "Evidently it's a rush job and the customer is paying extra for them to finish quickly. He said he'd come by later, in time to help with the pony rides."

"I'll make a start on the dishes," Gaby said, standing. "The meal was delicious."

Gran stood and they both started to clear the dishes. Her grandmother waited until they were both alone in the kitchen before she started talking. "How is the testing going? Do you have the reports back yet?"

"Only about half so far." Gaby tossed her grandmother a saucy grin. "Have you tested them yet?"

"Mother!" Gaby's mother overheard as she stepped into the kitchen. "This is your fault. I don't know why you can't confine your activities to normal ones." She rolled her eyes upward as if seeking heavenly aid. "Most people have normal parents who like to babysit their grandchildren and attend the Women's Division meetings. I'm stuck with one who discusses condoms and sex."

"Pooh." Gaby's grandmother flapped her right hand. "Where's the fun in normal?"

"Fancy Free is disgusting," Elsa said, entering the kitchen. "You have no idea of the embarrassment you cause me in the *Sloan Gazette* offices. People are always asking nosy questions about you both."

"Fancy Free brings lots of business to town and helps the local job situation," Gran said, narrowing her eyes and clearly ready to do battle.

Gaby hurriedly changed the subject because her grandmother was winding up an impressive head of steam. "What would you like me to do to help? Once we've done with the dishes, I mean."

"I haven't had a chance to ice the cupcakes," Elsa said, her tone grudging.

"I'm on it," Gaby said as the doorbell rang. "Why don't you go and relax with your guests and watch the kids. Gran and I will sort out the cupcakes. Do you want the sausage rolls heated too?"

Elsa's shoulders relaxed, some of the tension seeping out

of her. "Thanks. Could you put the sausage rolls on in half an hour?"

"Sure thing. If there's anything else you'd like us to do, shout out." Gaby glanced at the table of food with several large covered platters ready to serve to the guests. "You've been busy and deserve a break."

Gaby turned back to the sink and rinsed off several of the dinner plates ready to stack in the dishwasher. Her mother and Elsa both left the kitchen, leaving her with Gran.

"Don't let Elsa wind you up, Gran. She and Mum will never agree with our point of view."

"They're old fuddy-duddies," Gran snapped. "I'm sure they swapped my baby at birth," she added in a peeved tone.

"I don't think so, Gran. I've seen the photos of you when you were younger. You and Mum look like sisters."

"Humph."

Gaby grinned and continued to clear the dishes.

"Are you still doing your testing with Marc?"

Gaby paused to glance at her grandmother. Her stomach bucked yet she wouldn't lie since Gran had asked her a direct question. "No."

"Oh?" Gran's brows rose. "But you are testing the products with a man?"

"Yes." Gaby grabbed a handful of the cutlery and poked

the knives and forks into the holder in the dishwasher.

"I haven't seen you with anyone except Liam and Fletch..." Gran trailed off and Gaby could feel the speculative gaze on her back. "Which one are you sleeping with? They're both nice boys. Very sexy butts."

"Gran!" Gaby turned to face her unrepentant grandmother.

"I'm in the sex industry," Gran said, a twinkle in her eyes. "I'm not a nun, you know. Which one are you sleeping with? Liam or Fletch?"

"Um..." Something in her face must have given her away.

Gran's brows drew together. "Both of them?"

Heat stole into Gaby's face. "Yes."

"Hmm, how does that work? Do you have alternative nights?"

"Not exactly. Ah, I guess I'll need to make some icing. Where does Elsa keep the confectioner's sugar?"

"Don't change the subject, my girl. What do you mean not exactly? Do you mean the three of you?" Gran cast a swift glance at the door and lowered her voice. "One of those ménage a trois?"

"Yes."

"Well, isn't that interesting? I'm betting your mother doesn't realize."

"Of course not. She was mortified when I moved in with

Fletch and Liam. It was only when she saw we had separate rooms that she could look her friends in the face."

"I almost wish I could tell her," Gran said with real regret in her voice. "Still." She perked up noticeably. "I have a secret and she doesn't. That's enough for now. Is this a casual thing or something more serious?"

Gaby stopped to consider the question. "I don't know."

"Is it fun?"

"Fletch and Liam are great. They're my best friends."

"Jack is my best friend," Gran said. "Not for one day have I regretted marrying him. He's brilliant about helping me test products too. He—"

"Gran, I don't need those sorts of details. That's why I make sure you guys leave your names off the questionnaires."

"How is the sex?"

Gran was trying to embarrass her and enjoying every moment. It wouldn't work. "The sex is incredible, especially with both men focusing on me."

The rustle of clothing grabbed their attention and seconds later, Elsa rushed into the kitchen. "How are the sausage rolls going? I don't believe it. You haven't even put them in the oven yet."

"For some reason the oven is taking a while to heat up." The temperature light clicked off. "There. We'll pop them in now," Gaby said, striving for reassurance. She didn't want her sister to lose her temper.

"We have everything under control," Gran said, shooing Elsa from the kitchen.

Gaby popped the tray of sausage rolls into the oven and set the timer. "Do you think she heard me?"

"Nah." Gran dismissed Gaby's concerns. "She would've shrieked like a banshee if she'd overheard that juicy tidbit. I can't wait to tell Katarina."

"Gran, this info is personal. Private. No one needs to know except Fletch, Liam and me."

"Oh pooh," Gran said. "Spoilsport."

THE HOUSE WAS QUIET when Gaby let herself in the front door and disappointment struck hard. Still, it was only seven. The boys had probably gone out for a run or a drink at the Cricket. She could always head to the pub and seek them out. Even if they weren't there, she was bound to find one of her friends to spend time with and chill.

A yawn took her by surprise. Maybe not.

Boy, she was tired. Most of it was stress from biting her tongue during the birthday party and prior family dinner. In the lounge, she kicked off her shoes and ambled barefooted down the passage to her bedroom. The door to Fletch's bedroom was open and she glanced in, coming to an abrupt halt.

Fletch and Liam were lying on the bed, both naked, their arms wrapped around each other as they slept. A pang struck her. Loneliness maybe. She continued on to her bedroom, intending to pull on a pair of jeans and a T-shirt and kick back in front of the telly. Maybe she'd watch a movie. It wouldn't matter if she fell asleep.

"Gaby, sweetheart. Is that you?" Fletch called.

"Yeah, I just got back from the party."

"Why are you hiding out there?"

Because uncertainty had struck, along with a complicated emotion that came surprisingly close to jealousy. "I didn't want to disturb you."

There was silence then masculine murmurs. Fletch appeared in the doorway of her bedroom, naked with his dark hair sticking up in all directions. Despite his tiredness, he appeared happy and relaxed, as if he'd experienced good sex. Her mind skittered away from the subject, but the buck in her gut told the truth. She was envious of their closeness and feeling left out. "You wouldn't be disturbing us. You look tired and stressed. Come to bed with us." He stretched out his hand and waited.

She shifted her weight, hesitating. This thing between

them wasn't about comfort or sex for pure pleasure. They were helping her to test her inventions and choose the right one to market for Christmas. It wasn't about cementing a bond.

Gaby stared at his hand before scanning his expression. He smiled and waited patiently.

"I'll join you once I get undressed."

Fletch dropped his hand and stepped into her room. "Let me."

"Don't be silly. I can do it." Giving him permission to undress her was a step too far into intimacy. It felt like a betrayal of her feelings for Marc, hopeless as they were.

"Are you frightened of me?"

"Of course not."

Fletch turned on the charm, the dimples at the corner of his mouth deepening. "Let me fulfil a fantasy. Let me undress you."

"I'm your roomie, your friend."

"You're also our lover," Fletch said, unperturbed by her objections.

The trepidation inside her dispersed a fraction. It was difficult to forget the pleasure of being with both of them. It had seemed easy and natural. Better than she'd ever imagined. "All right." She held her ground when he moved closer. He smelled of male musk and sex all wrapped up with a tinge of his citrus shower gel. Perfect. Just one whiff let the residual tension seep from her muscles.

"You look pretty in this dress, Gaby." He smoothed one forefinger along the neckline, the faint drag of his finger sending her pulse leaping. She should throw her hands up in horror and shove him away. Heck, she should pack her bags and move out since their home had become an actual house of sin rather than the make-believe one of her mother's fertile imagination.

"Thanks."

"Turn around and let me get the zip for you."

Like a puppet, she turned at his bidding. The zipper glided downward with a whisper and the silky fabric of her dress slid down her arms. Under his guidance, the fabric whooshed over her hips, puddling at her feet like a colorful sunset.

"Hold on to my arm and step out of your dress," he said.

Gaby followed his instructions without hesitation, but inside her mind and body rioted. Her mind veered toward the sensible while her body cried out for Fletch's touch. Her breasts swelled against the lace of her bra and distinct moisture gathered between her legs.

"Can I loosen your hair?"

"Yes." Her acknowledgment was scarcely more than a whisper. It was seduction plain and simple, and she faltered, helpless against his determined charm.

Competent fingers tugged the combs and clips from her hair until it fell around her shoulders in a perfumed curtain. Fletch lifted a lock to his nose and inhaled. "Beautiful. I like the way you smell. It's classy yet sexy. Subtle. I like subtle." He glanced down at her panties and smirked. "I bet your mother didn't realize what you were wearing beneath your dress."

"What's wrong with my lingerie?" Fletch was too perceptive for his own good. She'd dressed with Liam and Fletch in mind, a small act of disobedience when she knew her mother and sister would needle her about her chosen occupation yet again. She sighed. She should be used to their verbal zingers, but each time her mother and sister put her down, they hurt her. "Tell me."

"Not a thing is wrong. It's perfect to showcase your gorgeous body."

The heat in his eyes made her feel beautiful. Special.

He cupped one breast and her breath caught—the warmth from his hand like a brand. Her head rolled back and her eyelids slid to half-mast to better concentrate on the sensations he was evoking in her. His fingers tightened on her nipple, focusing her thoughts on the sliver of pain. A shiver rolled over her. How did he know exactly what she liked?

"As pretty as these are, I want to take them off." His hands slipped behind her back and twisted, releasing her bra before she could blink.

"You've done that before."

"A time or two," he admitted.

She'd seen him with women, some her friends and some not. Fletch never talked about his sexual exploits. Liam didn't either. They didn't bring women back to the house and, not for the first time, she wondered why. "How come you never bring women home with you? Liam doesn't either."

"Bringing a woman into our home gives them ideas. I can't speak for Liam, but I haven't met anyone I wanted to encourage in that way."

"Oh." Which begged all sorts of questions about her role in their home. Once she'd fit the friend box and it had seemed natural. Now the rules had changed and she wasn't sure how to act.

He slipped her bra down her arms and tossed it on the bed beside the dress. Then he turned to her, his gaze doing a sweep of her upper torso and ending at her breasts. They prickled as if he were touching her, running his callused fingers over her curves. Her nipples stiffened, and she fought the shyness that jumped out of nowhere.

This...thing with Fletch and Liam...it was taking her

places she hadn't expected to travel, making her reexamine everything she'd thought about herself.

Fletch's expression softened and he drew her into his arms. Before she summoned her wits to ask him what he was doing, he was kissing her. She froze for an instant before his persuasive lips drove away every thought of protest. He cradled her head gently, alternating passionate kisses with quick sips that slowly drove her to the point of madness. With a sigh of surrender, she wound her arms around his neck and hung on to enjoy the ride. He slipped a hand between them to thumb one nipple, and a tingle sprang to life in her pussy.

One touch and he made her wetter, yearning for his possession.

She almost cried when he lifted his head and stepped away.

"Let's go to bed," he said, capturing her hand and tugging Gaby from her bedroom.

In his bedroom, he scooped her off her feet and placed her beside Liam before following her down. He had an erection, yet it didn't appear to bother him, flaunting his dick with carefree ease.

"Can I take your panties off for you now?"

Gaby bit back a giggle. "You have a panty fetish?"

"Only for yours."

She relaxed as he moved down the bed, lifting her hips at his silent urging. He slid the filmy garment down her legs and tossed it aside.

"Can I taste you?"

"Yes." This wasn't testing her toys, a small voice reminded her. She was about to take back her agreement when his tongue slid the length of her slit. An explosion of hunger hit her and she melted into the mattress, letting him do his worst. A startled hiss escaped her. The man had skills. With leisurely laps, he moved up and down until fire streaked through her. He fluttered his tongue over her clit, sending pleasure sailing free. She let out a soft cry and he immediately intensified his attention to her clit. He surrounded the engorged bud with his lips, lapping and teasing until she finally exploded into a toe-curling climax.

When her quivers finally subsided, he rose up the bed and kissed her. A gentle caress of lips. She tasted her tart juices on his mouth and sighed. The perfect way to relieve stress.

"Can I fuck you, sweetheart?"

How could she say no? "Yes." She longed for a hard cock to fill her and drive away the emptiness left by the visit to her family. If it weren't for her father and her grandparents, she wouldn't visit the family home as often.

Fletch reached for a bedside drawer and pulled out a box.

He shook it and frowned. "Damn, we've used all the test condoms. Do you have some in your bedroom?"

"Probably. Wait." She grabbed his arm before he could jump from the bed. "Remember, I'm on the Pill. You don't need to use a condom."

Fletch froze, his eyes darkening with emotion. "You sure?"

"Yes." She trusted him implicitly. Liam too. She smiled encouragement. "You can be my first. I've never had sex without using a condom."

"Me neither."

"Well then." She swallowed, aware that, once again, she was annihilating her list of unofficial rules, yet this felt right. Gaby reached for him in silent encouragement, elated when he returned to her side.

"If you're positive."

"I am," she whispered.

He kissed her before he rose over her. She held her breath as he slowly pushed into her. Moist tissues parted as he slid home and her breath eased out. Perfect. So perfect. She could feel his heat, and as he withdrew and thrust into her again, a shimmer of delight slid across her nerve endings. Their lips met and she melted into his embrace. The coil of energy in her lower body grew with each unhurried thrust. When his lips fastened on her neck and he sucked, a bungee of pleasure slammed her. Then he braced his weight on his shoulders and increased his pace. Hard and fast thrusts that rattled the bed and pushed her over into orgasm in seconds flat. With satisfaction still pulsing through her, she reached up to apply her mouth to his nipple. She licked, sucked and bit him lightly.

Fletch cursed, and she froze.

"Do it again," Liam whispered from her other side. "He likes a hint of pain too."

Taking Liam at his word, she repeated the action. Fletch groaned, thrust hard and stilled, coming so hard she felt the pulse of his cock, the splash of his seed as he climaxed. Gradually, he relaxed and he lowered his head to kiss her.

"Thank you. That was amazing." He pulled out of her and kissed her again.

"Don't I get a kiss?" Liam asked.

Gaby gasped, but Fletch didn't hesitate. He leaned over and kissed Liam, an unhurried meeting of lips, before pulling back with a grin.

"It's getting cold," Liam said. "I'm knackered." He stood to pull back the covers and slid beneath. "Let's get some sleep."

Confusion struck Gaby over the head. They were sleeping together now? All of them? She glanced away from Liam to catch Fletch studying her reaction.

"Spend the night with us, Gaby."

"It's early."

"So? Liam and I had a hard day."

"I'll just clean up." Gaby scuttled from the bed as if monsters chased her. Good analogy. She felt as if something large and scary dogged her heels. The haunting started the first night when she'd trespassed into lover territory. In the bathroom, she cleaned up and used a cream to wipe away her makeup.

Ten minutes later, she dithered in the passage outside Fletch's bedroom. She peeked around the corner and saw the two men under the covers, lying so close she knew they must be touching. She started to walk past then retreated and marched into Fletch's room.

Liam opened one eye to peer blearily at her. "Coming in?"

"Yeah." She slipped under the covers and cuddled against Liam's warm body. It didn't feel wrong or weird or anything else except perfect. Gaby went to sleep with a smile on her face.

Chapter Nine

A few days later

Gaby stared into her morning cup of coffee. She was dressed, ready to go to work, yet she continued to sit at the breakfast table, stalling.

Liam put a hand on her arm and squeezed lightly. "A penny for them."

"Don't forget to account for inflation and the two and a half percent hike in GST," Fletch said. "I bid a dollar."

"The board meeting to give the go-ahead for my designs is this morning. I'm..." She trailed off with a shrug, not wanting to admit her nerves.

"You're worried," Liam said.

Her spine hit the back of the chair. "I'm not." But she was because she'd poured her heart and soul into this design, taken a chance to approach Alice and James to get the go-ahead for testing.

"Don't you think Liam and I get nervous when we put

in our building tenders and wait for the result? Of course we do. It's natural after you put so much into a project."

"Your vibrator design is top-notch, Gaby. Fancy Free is lucky to have you working for them," Liam added his words of support to Fletch's. "You're gonna kick butt today." He stood. "It's time for you to go."

Doubt demons whispered in Gaby's ears. She wasn't as sure of the outcome, but Liam was right. She needed to go because she was already late. She stood and reached for her briefcase and her car keys.

"Wait," Liam said, grasping her shoulder and tugging her to face him. "You need a good-luck kiss." He glanced at Fletch. "Two should do the trick."

Before she could move, he lowered his head and claimed her lips. It wasn't the quick brush of lips she expected. Her mouth parted and their lips and tongues did the mambo. When they finally parted, they were both breathing heavily.

"My turn," Fletch said.

His kiss was just as passionate—the kiss of a lover. He pulled away and shunted her gently toward the door. "Good luck."

"Break a leg," Liam added.

In a daze, Gaby stumbled out to her car, warm and tingly thoughts rioting through her mind and echoing in her

SHELLEY MUNRO

body. No one had ever wished her luck like that. Fletch and Liam believed in her, and it was heady stuff.

When Gaby walked into the boardroom, everyone was already present and they'd been there for a while. The empty cake plate bore witness to the fact.

"You couldn't have saved me a piece of cake?" She wet her finger and tapped a crumb before lifting it to her mouth. "Coffee cake. My favorite."

"You shouldn't have slept late." Richard popped the last bite into his mouth without a hint of apology.

"Leave the girl alone," Alice said as Gaby slipped onto a seat between her and Richard. "She's innovative. An absolute genius at design."

Pleasure surged through Gaby and for a change it wasn't sexual. "Do you have a favorite?"

"The vibrator that fits with the music player. It's amazing the way the vibrations vary with the music. I tried it alone and with James. Women will kill to own one of these."

Her grandmother's knitting needles paused mid-row. "She has dollar signs in her eyes."

"Which did you prefer?" Alice asked.

"The same one as you." Her grandmother leaned closer to whisper, "The orgasms were spectacular."

Gaby laughed and tried not to picture her grandparents

in bed. "Good to hear."

James rushed in to join them. "Sorry about the wait. I had to take a phone call. All right. Preliminary findings. Gaby?"

Gaby rose, not needing to refer to the notes she'd brought with her. She'd glanced through the reports from the professional testers Fancy Free hired on arrival at work. So far, everyone was overwhelmingly in favor of the vibrator, although the musical butt plug was also popular. "Most of our testers have positive feedback about the vibrator and everyone liked the musical attachment. There have also been positive comments about the butt plugs as well. Does anyone have any questions or comments about any of the products?"

"I think we have a winner," Alice said. "I liked the vibrator because I could vary the sensations by using different attachments. It's fun having something available to fit my mood, be it fast and furious or slow and leisurely."

Katarina nodded emphatically. "I thought they'd feel awkward, but I liked the materials you used to make them. I found the attachments easy to change."

"They weren't too fiddly for my old hands," Ben added.

"This is what we should do," Alice said. "Market the vibrator with a basic attachment and offer the other attachments as extras. Maybe run a special for a limited time—two attachments for the price of one. The musical butt plug also impressed me. Maybe we could save that for a promotion for Valentine's day, repeating the vibrator and including the butt plug for those who are more adventurous."

"Brilliant," Gran said, turning her knitting around to start another row.

Ben offered a thumbs-up. "You've got yourself a clever wife there, James."

"I know." James's voice sounded smug and proud, and Gaby suffered a twinge of envy until she recalled the kisses she'd received from Liam and Fletch this morning. They'd told her she had no worries and would kick butt. They'd sent her off to work feeling positive about her abilities. In the past, the only people to encourage her in that manner were her father and grandparents. With Marc, there'd always been an unspoken rivalry.

James glanced at each of those present at the meeting. "Does everyone agree with Alice? And do we need to tweak the product to improve it?"

"Can we do a deal with a music company to give the product extra value?" Richard asked.

"Excellent idea," Alice said. "I'll get right on research for that."

Gaby almost laughed out loud at the chagrined

ROMP

expressions from the rest of the elderly board members. They were a competitive lot and liked to come up with useable ideas.

Katarina brightened visibly. "Group the songs in packages. One for romantic. One for rough and ready. One for fast and furious. That sort of thing."

Alice scribbled another note.

"Fast and furious?" Ben asked in an incredulous tone. "What's that song about a slow hand?"

Sam dragged his fingers through his sparse hair, appearing perplexed. "Yeah, I thought you women liked to get revved up. Leastways that's what my wife told me."

"Haven't you ever done it up against a door?" Richard asked.

James and Alice exchanged a grin.

"Details," Gaby said promptly.

"I'll tell you personal details about my love life when you tell me about yours," Richard replied, the glint of challenge in his eyes. He had her there.

"I've done it on a beach," Gran said. "Sand gets in your hoo-ha. So much sand I was still finding the stuff in the shower a week later."

Gaby spluttered, imagining the scenario all too well.

"You had sex in a public place?" Sam asked the question.

Gran paused mid-row. "I don't like bedroom antics to

147

get stale."

"You should try it on a spaceship," Richard muttered under his breath.

A spaceship? Gaby frowned, but none of the others had heard him. Surely, he was joking?

Sam turned to Gaby in open curiosity. "What do you young people do?"

"Yeah," Katarina said. "Is there some place we should try to keep up with the fashion?"

Gaby did a credible fish impression while trying to think of a suitable reply. None of the elderly board members interrupted. Instead they waited for her to speak. "What's wrong with a bed?" she asked finally. A nice soft bed worked for her, especially if there were two men stretched between the sheets. The longer they stared, the greater the heat suffusing her cheeks.

"She's blushing," James said.

Which, of course, made her blush worse. Another first.

"Do you have a secret?" Gran asked, her tone verging on sly.

"No, of course not."

"The swimming hole is a good spot," Alice said, thankfully taking the heat off her. "The bed and breakfast," she added with a wink at James.

"Outside, under the stars is good if it's a warm summer

night. My arthritis starts playing up if it's too cold," Ben said.

"Anyone joined the Mile High Club?" Distraction. Her grandmother was still staring at her, looking as if she wanted to ask questions and provide more discussion for everyone.

"Yes," Richard said.

"As much as this conversation is fascinating, does Gaby need to change anything on the design?" James broke in before the oldies could add more input.

"No," Gran said instantly.

"It's perfect," Alice said.

"The instructions were clear." Ben set down his coffee mug. "But we should tart them up a bit and add some sexy tips to romance your partner."

"Perfect," Alice agreed. "Excellent suggestion. James and I can work on that."

"Any other questions or concerns?" James asked.

Gaby held her breath, excitement fizzing inside her like a glass of expensive champagne.

"Does anyone want to suggest a final color?" Alice asked.

"Christmas colors," Katarina said firmly. "Red, green and maybe some stylish gold writing. We could package them in gold boxes with red and green ribbons."

"We don't want them to look too gimmicky," Gaby

protested. The last thing she wanted was for her product to fail because people hated the colors.

"Don't worry," Alice said. "I have just the right color palette in mind. Come with me after the meeting and I'll show you."

"Good," James said. "I think we're done here."

Gaby followed Alice from the boardroom as the oldies burst into chatter. Gran's loud voice followed her down the passage, demanding to hear details about the Mile High Club because she wanted to join too.

Alice giggled. "You're lucky to have such a progressive grandmother."

"She has her moments," Gaby said. "My mother isn't quite as supportive of my career choice."

Alice took her arm and towed Gaby into her office. "Don't worry about their opinions. You have friends here. My parents don't tell their friends about my occupation and James' mother and sister are plain horrid about Fancy Free."

Gaby sighed. "I know the feeling. My mother and sister give me a hard time."

"Don't listen to them. Your designs make a lot of people—both men and women—happy. And we couldn't do without you. You're an integral part of our team."

In her office, Alice unlocked a cupboard and pulled out a

storyboard along with color swatches. "James and I were so pleased and excited by the product we spent the weekend brainstorming marketing ideas and colors."

Pleasure suffused Gaby. They'd liked her designs and hadn't waited for the board to confirm the project. She ran her gaze over the storyboard.

Christmas is Coming, the title screamed.

The board contained her instructions on how to use the different attachments plus tips on making Christmas a romantic holiday. Gaby's throat tightened and her eyes misted over. It was perfect. Absolutely perfect.

"You've put a lot of work into this. Our advertising team couldn't do better."

Alice beamed. "We're thrilled with the design, and we're proud of you." She pulled a box out of the cupboard and handed it to Gaby. "This is something small to let you know how much we appreciate the work you put into this design. We realize you worked a lot of unpaid hours, which is why we intend to give you a large Christmas bonus. This design is a winner, and I don't know how you're going to top your vibrator."

Five minutes later, Gaby left Alice's office in a daze, the gift-wrapped box clutched in her right hand.

Down in the lab she shared with Marc, she settled at her desk and opened one end of the parcel Alice had given her.

Champagne. The good French stuff. She knew just the two men to help her celebrate. Smiling, she set the package aside and checked her emails before plunging into work on a new ultrathin condom design. Alice and James wanted something strong and even thinner than their current best seller. She stood to grab a lab coat off the hook by her desk. She shrugged into it, fastening several buttons to keep the coat from flapping open.

She walked over to her testing station and made a halfhearted attempt to start. Unable to settle, she returned to her desk and picked up her cell phone to ring Fletch.

"Gaby? Something wrong?" Fletch asked.

Gaby heard Liam's voice in the background. "No, nothing wrong. They liked my design for the vibrator. It's going into production for the Christmas market."

He let out a celebratory shout. "Awesome, sweetheart. Not that I'm surprised."

Liam said something else and Fletch told him her news. "Gaby?"

Liam had taken possession of the phone. "We're taking you out to dinner tonight. We'll go somewhere special."

Gaby grinned. "Sounds great."

"And we'll have a private celebration," Fletch said loudly in the background.

"Count on it," Liam added.

They said their goodbyes and Gaby hung up with the promise of a fun, sexy evening shimmering in front of her.

Marc sauntered into the lab. "Gaby, I have a prototype for a new condom. Do you have time to test it with me?" He waggled his brows up and down in a suggestive manner. "Can I get into your pants?"

Gaby didn't take time to consider her answer. "You'll have to ask one of the test team to help you." Surprise—no, shock—filled her as she uttered the words. A week ago she'd thought she'd loved Marc, and now she wasn't blind to his faults. The man was obsessed with his work. He lived and breathed his designs.

While she loved her job, she wanted a personal life too.

"Damn, is it your time of the month?"

Gaby's eyes widened. "I can't believe you just said that."

"You've never said no before, not unless you had your period and didn't feel like sex. What am I meant to think?"

Great, now he sounded indignant. And, if she was fair, she did hold a portion of the blame. "I'm sorry. It doesn't feel right having sex with you now that I'm with someone else, not even work-related sex for testing condoms."

"I'm sorry to hear that." His top lip curled. "Selfish, I know, but it was always fun with you."

She listened to herself speak, even heard Marc's smiling reply and registered the wry twist of lips. But at the same time, her mind roared at her. She'd been sleeping with Fletch and Liam for around a week. Somewhere along the way, she'd decided to keep them.

They'd agreed to help her test her designs.

That was all.

Neither of them had hinted anything more could come of their agreement.

"I'd better get to work on this design or Alice and James will sack me."

"Sure thing." With a wave, Marc wandered from the lab, his white lab coat flapping around his legs.

Gaby's mind returned to the successful board meeting. With the testing completed, she didn't need Fletch and Liam to help her any longer. Goal achieved, so why had the fizz seeped out of her happy mood?

Chapter Ten

LIAM'S CELL PHONE VIBRATED and he paused his hammering to check the screen. Rachel. Again.

"Problem?" Fletch asked.

"Rachel is ringing me again."

"Didn't you ring her back the other day?"

"Someone distracted me," Liam said drily, part of him surprised he could actually talk about sex with his friend without stammering. Mindful of a couple of their workers within earshot, he didn't add anything else.

"Ring her back now. Signal me if you need an interruption."

Nodding, Liam hit dial. "Hi, Rachel. What's up?"

"Where have you been? I've been trying to reach you since the weekend." Her voice measured a register only slightly less than a screech.

Liam scowled and held the phone farther from his ear.

"I've been busy." Damn if he intended to apologize. He was glad he hadn't asked her out again. While they'd had an agreeable time during their two outings, and they'd ended up in bed after the second one, he hadn't wanted her enough to follow-up for another date.

"Too busy to spare a few minutes?"

Liam didn't bother answering her accusation. He didn't owe her explanations. His gut instinct had warned him beforehand and he'd made a point of telling her their sleeping together was a one-off. He hadn't wanted to treat her like a commodity.

"We need to talk."

"I don't think so."

"Wait! Don't hang up. I'll meet you at the cafe. You have to eat, right? Can you spare half an hour around midday?"

Liam got the idea she'd keep pestering him until he agreed. "All right," he said grudgingly. "Midday at the cafe."

"See you then." Rachel disconnected the call.

"What was that about?" Fletch asked.

"She wants to meet me at the cafe."

"She's pregnant."

"Not by me, she isn't. We used a condom and it worked perfectly."

"Is it wrong of me to feel jealous?"

"Jesus." Liam glanced around to see if any of their workers were eavesdropping. "Not at work."

"But we can at home?"

"Yes." Hell, agreement had come so easily, yet with Rachel he wanted to run a mile, and preferably toward Fletch and Gaby. Thinking about the implications of this made his head hurt. "I don't suppose you're free for lunch today."

Fletch smirked. "As it happens I have an opening in my calendar. It's a date."

Liam's teeth ground together. "Fletch."

"I'll behave. Promise." Sincerity glowed on his face and Liam relaxed.

"I wonder what she wants."

"Only time will tell. Let's get this frame finished," Fletch said.

Three hours later, he and Fletch entered the Sloan cafe.

"Do you see her?" Fletch asked.

"Yeah, she's sitting in the far corner. Food first or go and see what she wants?"

"Talk to her first. We might want to leave."

"Good point." No matter how Liam studied this situation, his gut bucked with trepidation. What the hell did the woman want? If she thought she was going to pressure him into a permanent relationship, she needed to rethink her strategy. He strode over to the corner table, aware of Fletch at his heels.

"Did you have to bring him?" Rachel narrowed her bright blue eyes and tucked a strand of blonde hair behind her ear.

"We both needed to eat," Liam said.

"What I have to say to you is private."

Fletch shrugged. "No problem. Liam, should I order you coffee and something to eat?"

"Better get it to go," Liam said. "We don't want to be late to our meeting with the suppliers."

Fletch ambled off, leaving them alone. Liam took a second to appreciate the view before turning back to Rachel. "What's so important for you to hound me for days?"

Stung by his words, she glared. "If you'd returned my call, I wouldn't have needed to hassle you."

"Clock's ticking." Dammit. He didn't usually act with cruelty. "I'm sorry. We're busy at present and have deadlines to meet. How can I help you?"

"I'm pregnant. You're the father."

Liam stared at her. "Me?"

"Yeah, isn't it great? You're gonna be a father." She grinned at him. "We need to talk about wedding dates. We have a lot to do. We don't want our baby coming into the world without—"

"Wait! No way. We only had sex once."

Some of the happy glow left Rachel. "Pregnancy only takes one time."

"We used a condom."

"Condoms aren't one hundred percent effective. You know that." Rachel pulled a small diary from her handbag. "We can get married next month."

Panic struck Liam, robbing him of speech. He let her prattle on about churches and dresses and bridesmaids.

"Liam?" Rachel finally realized he wasn't listening to her.

"I'm not marrying you." No way did he want to marry Rachel. Gaby and Fletch... No!

"But you have to." This time Rachel was the one to show alarm.

"No, I don't. You can't make me. If the baby is mine, I'll support you in any way I can, but I won't marry you."

"You'd walk away from your own child?" Moisture welled in her eyes until a tear rolled down her cheek. She looked pretty when she cried. Most women didn't. "I thought you of all people would understand and want to provide your child with a stable upbringing. I can't believe you're denying everything."

"Because my mother was the town tramp and I have

no idea of the identity of my father? Think again." Liam stood, desperate to get away from her.

"But we're having a child."

"And I told you if the baby's mine I'll support you financially. I have to go." He strode from the cafe into the sunshine, ignoring the interest of the other customers.

"Liam! Wait up."

Liam slowed his steps for Fletch to catch up. "You heard?"

"Everyone in the cafe heard. You realize you're going to be the bad guy in all this? People will say you take after your father. They'll dredge up stories about your mother again."

"Yeah." Liam stopped to rub his hand over his face. "Big difference though. My father walked away without looking back. I offered to support her. Fletch, I can't marry her. I can't, not when you and Gaby..." He trailed off, unable to voice his feelings or his fears.

"I get it." Fletch squeezed his shoulder in silent support. "You were kinder to her than I would've been. Who was she going out with before you? How do we know she's not trying to stick you with someone else's baby?"

"That was my first thought. Hell, maybe I'm being unfair and she is carrying my baby."

"She can't make you marry her."

"Her father will come after me with a shotgun."

"They don't have shotgun weddings anymore. You gonna tell Gaby?"

"I wouldn't hide something like this from either of you." Liam checked for interested bystanders. "Even if we weren't sleeping together, I would've told you both. You're my best friends."

THE OLD INN WAS English in style, quiet and elegant and perfect for their first date. Gaby smiled at the idea because it was a date even though there were three of them.

Liam had booked a private table, one overlooking the cottage garden in the courtyard at the back of the restaurant. They'd dressed for the occasion. She wore another dress—this one black and white—while Liam and Fletch wore black trousers and nice shirts. Liam wore pale blue while Fletch wore cream.

"Hi, Tina," Fletch said to the waitress. She was Katarina's granddaughter and a few years younger than Gaby. "We have a table booked."

"Are you celebrating something special?"

"We are," Liam said. "Gaby has some good work news." He tapped his nose as he grinned at Tina. "It's top secret."

"That must be why Nana and Granddad said they couldn't come to dinner the other night." She giggled. "They make me laugh with their secret squirrel stuff. This way. I saved the table you requested." She showed them over to the table and once they were seated, handed them menus and a wine list before bustling away to attend to new arrivals.

Gaby scanned the menu and decided to order the fish of the day—blue cod—plus a salad.

"I'm having the rack of lamb," Fletch said.

"Me too," Liam said. "You guys want wine?"

Fletch set the menu down. "Nope. I'm gonna have a beer."

"I'll have a glass of wine," Gaby said. "Alice and James gave me a bottle of French champagne today. It's in the fridge chilling."

"French champagne?" Fletch whistled. "That's too good to waste on me."

"I can't think of more perfect people to share it with." Gaby leaned closer to whisper. "We don't have to drink champagne out of glasses you know."

A noticeable shudder went through Fletch, and Gaby winked at Liam.

"You've hooked him," Liam said.

"It's a date." Fletch's voice was husky with promise.

"Damn, is it hot in here?"

"Guess what we talked about at the board meeting today?" Gaby knew they'd never guess.

"Tell us," Liam said.

"Sex in a public place."

A wicked smirk crawled across Fletch's face. "You can grope me under the table. Either of you, but I'm not taking off my clothes for everyone here to watch."

"I don't think that's the sort of public place they had in mind," Liam said. "I've had sex at the swimming hole and once when I went camping with my girlfriend at the time."

"Sounds like fun," Fletch said. "We'll have to keep those locations in mind."

"As long as we don't do it on the beach," Gaby said. "I have it on good authority I'll get sand in my hoo-ha."

Fletch's guffaw broke off abruptly. "Aw, hell. Guess who just walked in with her parents?"

Liam groaned. "Rachel?"

"Got it in one," Gaby said. "She was hot and heavy with Bryce Ross, not so long ago. You really think she's telling the truth?"

A heavy sigh came from deep in Liam's chest. "It's possible I'm the father, but if she thinks she can trap me into marriage, she should rethink her plans. A baby isn't a good excuse to get married these days."

"Didn't Bryce shoot through in the middle of the night, disappearing from town and leaving a heap of debts?" Fletch asked.

Liam spoke in a low voice. "The gossip mill said he'd pulled a swifty on Rachel's father, stealing and on selling a heap of supplies. He used to work for him."

"Fletch. Liam." Robert Scott, Rachel's father stopped by their table. "And it's Gabrielle, isn't it?"

"Gaby Montgomery, our house mate," Fletch said, completing the introductions.

"Liam. Fletch. I'm pleased to meet you, Gaby," Rachel's mother said.

Rachel remained silent but flashed a smile.

"Do you boys intend to put in a bid to work on the housing for the new subdivision?" Robert asked.

"We're hoping to take a look this week," Liam said. "We've been flat out finishing the Gibson house."

"You boys do good work," Robert said. "I'd like to award the contract to a local. If you have any questions, call me."

"Thanks, we'll do that," Fletch said.

"Enough business, Robert," Rachel's mother said. "Let these people enjoy their dinner."

"I'll look forward to your bid," Robert said, and with a wave they left to go to their assigned table.

"Rachel's parents don't know about the baby yet," Gaby

said.

"Doesn't seem like it," Fletch said.

Liam frowned, his blue eyes swirling with emotion. "The contract for the subdivision is a huge one. It would set us up with work for the next eighteen months. If, or rather when, Rachel decides to tell her parents, we can kiss any hope of getting the job goodbye."

"My thoughts exactly." Fletch reached over and placed his hand over Liam's, squeezing lightly. "Don't worry about it. There's lots of work around at present. If we don't get this contract, we'll get something else."

The waitress arrived to take their order, and they relaxed, the chat flowing as it usually did between them. The meal was amazing and Gaby couldn't remember enjoying herself on a date as much as she did with Fletch and Liam.

Back at the house, Liam opened the champagne. "A toast," he said. "To Gaby and her amazing inventions."

"To Gaby," Fletch echoed.

"I want to thank you both for helping me test my designs."

"Anytime, sweetheart," Fletch said.

"It was a real hardship," Liam added with a smirk. "We're available anytime you need help with testing."

But what about now? The question tickled the tip of her tongue, although she wasn't brave enough to voice it aloud. *Coward*.

"We should adjourn to the bedroom," Fletch said.

"Gaby?" Liam scrutinized her as closely as Fletch, neither saying a word while they waited for her decision.

Gaby picked up her glass. "I thought you'd never ask."

Fletch took her free hand in his and led her down the passage with Liam following close on their heels. As usual, they ended up in Fletch's room. The master bedroom had become their room by default.

"Off with your clothes." Fletch took the glass from her and set it, plus his, on the nightstand. He kicked off his shoes and socks and sprawled out on the bed. "Give us a show."

"Music?" Gaby was all for a striptease. An excellent way to rev the libido.

"Liam can sing."

Liam toed off his shoes, peeled off black socks and sprawled beside Fletch, their shoulders brushing with comforting familiarity. He started to sing an old rock classic, husky voice pitch-perfect while Fletch eyed her in expectation, a smile hovering around his sexy lips.

Right, they wanted a show. She'd give them one. She loved to dance.

She started with a slow rotation of hips, rocking to the beat of the song. Liam's voice strummed across her senses while the heat in her men's gazes thrilled her no end.

Her men?

Gaby faltered momentarily before picking up the beat again. Go with the flow and worry about the other stuff later. Her hips rocked. She shimmied and did a creditable pop diva strut before smoothly sliding down the side zipper of her dress. A wink and a sexy pout accompanied the subtle shoulder shrug that slid one side of her bodice down and bared the curve of a breast.

"I didn't notice she wasn't wearing a bra," Fletch said.

"I did." No mistaking Liam's sexy drawl for anything except suggestive.

"Keep singing," Fletch ordered. "Otherwise I'll have to start and that will really kill the mood."

Gaby shuddered and it had nothing to do with her partial undressed state. Fletch's singing sounded like a bullfrog on a bad day. She turned an imploring gaze on Liam. "He means it. Please don't subject us to that torture."

Liam hurriedly started singing again, laughter threading the husky lyrics of his chosen song.

She swayed, released her grip on her dress and, with a swivel of her hips, the fabric slid down, hitting the floor with a whoosh. Still rocking to the beat of Liam's song, she stepped out of the fabric.

"That's it," Fletch said. "I can't wait." He leaped off the bed, scooped her up and tossed her onto the mattress.

"Fletch! I haven't even had a chance to take off my shoes."

"No problem. We'll do it," Fletch said, sitting at the foot of the bed. He cradled one of her feet in his hand, his eyes gleaming with mischief. "Liam?"

"You're all on your own," Liam said. "I'm not the impatient one." He winked at her seconds before lowering his head to kiss her. And what a kiss. There were no preliminaries. It was the kiss of a man intent on sex, an experienced man who knew exactly what moves to make. A confident man. Gaby clung to him, enjoying the ride.

When Liam lifted his head and stared at her, the atmosphere thickened. A sharp tug on one foot made her glance at the foot of the bed.

"Hello? I'm here." Fletch's disgruntlement came through clearly.

A spurt of uncertainty grabbed her. How did they make this work without one of them feeling left out? She shot a quick look at Liam. His smile was reassuring, and he followed it up with another wink.

"Feeling left out?" he asked.

"Yes." Fletch unbuckled and removed both of her shoes as he spoke. He tossed them to the floor.

"Come up here." Liam bent to whisper in her ear, his sultry suggestion warming her inside and out. "Lose the clothes first," he added. "We have plans for you."

For once, Fletch seemed at a loss, his normal confidence absent. "What about you guys?"

"Our plans don't require us to lose all our clothes," Gaby said sweetly. "Hurry up. Time's a-wastin'."

Fletch stood and slowly removed his shirt, black trousers and underwear. "Should I be worried?"

Liam snorted. "Only if too much pleasure throws you. Stop being such a wimp."

Fletch crawled up the bed, and as soon as he was in range, they jumped him. Liam pushed him flat against the mattress while she went down to the business end. When she glanced up, she saw Liam kissing Fletch in the same way he'd kissed her.

The tension seeped out of Fletch, his taut muscles relaxing. Gaby couldn't tear her eyes off the two men. Their kiss was aggressive for the most part, but then Liam gentled the contact, seducing and cajoling a response. Fletch moaned and his arms wound around Liam, pulling him closer so their chests brushed.

A sigh whispered from Gaby and she fought the urge to finger herself. Need hummed through her, but she wanted to draw it out. Smiling, she trailed her hand over

Fletch's hipbone. His partial erection had filled out, his cock bobbing in the air.

Bending her head, she placed teasing kisses on his hip, gradually moving closer to his groin. She heard a moan, felt the shift in his breathing when she kissed his shaft and made a tiny, teasing foray with her tongue. His scent drifted over her as she tormented him. As much as her body clamored for action, this was right where she wanted to be—tormenting Fletch with Liam as her partner in crime.

She upped her tempo, swirling her warm, wet tongue over the head of his cock. His hips jerked, driving his shaft deeper into her mouth. Gaby went with the offer, tasting his pre-come and pulling out all stops to drive him crazy.

"Shift over."

Gaby's head lifted in surprise.

"He asked for some attention," Liam said.

Fletch's succinct curse would have made her mother tut. Gaby just grinned and shifted over to allow Liam access to Fletch. She cast a saucy grin at Fletch, noticed the faint color in his cheeks, his swollen lips and the heat in his brown eyes. They glowed with open need and desire, causing a spike of return heat in her.

"I need another kiss from you before we torture Fletch some more."

She sank into their kiss and gave in to the urge to touch. Her hand snaked under the band of her panties and between her legs, gliding across slick flesh. The zing of sensation made her gasp against Liam's lips. He drew back, his blue eyes sparkling with an echo of the desire she'd witnessed in Fletch.

"Just a little longer, Gaby. The wait will be worth it. Okay?"

"Yes." She didn't question Liam's right to order them around. He wasn't being obnoxious, and since the three of them had the same goal, Liam's taking control worked for her.

"Ready to put Fletch on edge?"

"Oh yes." Laughter filled her, silently bubbling like an effervescent drink. She felt giddy and excited as a world of possibilities opened to them. She bent her head, snatched another kiss from Liam then turned her attention to Fletch. As before she licked the head of Fletch's cock, but this time Liam joined her, his tongue flickering out to take a taste. Sometimes their tongues touched while at other times Fletch was their only connection. Their gazes caught and held, a link binding them together.

Fletch's groans and soft curses filled the air, his large frame quivering, his hips jerking upward as he attempted to find a mouth. Liam backed off, giving her a faint nod.

She took Fletch into her mouth while Liam tongued his balls and sac, his fingers roving over Fletch.

"Stop," Fletch said without warning. "I can't take much more."

Liam smirked at her, lifting his brows in a smug expression. "But you wanted attention."

"Smart-arse."

"You want to suck me off while you and Fletch do the regular thing?" Liam asked in an undertone.

"What are you two whispering about?"

"Nothing to concern you," Liam retorted, yanking at his remaining clothes.

Gaby gave a slight nod and stripped off her panties as well.

"Fletch, Gaby wants you to fuck her."

"Hallelujah!" Fletch rolled away from the middle of the mattress and patted the space he'd vacated. "Come on up, sweetheart. What are you going to do?"

Liam couldn't prevent a smirk at the suspicious note in Fletch's voice. "I'm going to watch and critique your performance." Although he aimed for impassive, his lips quivered.

"Fuck that." Fletch brushed an absent kiss on Gaby's shoulder while glaring at him.

"Isn't it me you're gonna fuck, Fletch?" A mischievous

note entered Gaby's voice and Liam wanted to laugh. Sex with Fletch and Gaby was a constant surprise and full of fun along with pleasure that rocked him soul-deep.

With a grumble, Fletch positioned himself and pushed inside Gaby. One thing Liam hadn't considered was how hot it would be watching instead of participating. It was easy to see Gaby got off on watching, and he could see why she liked seeing the sexual action.

"Wait!" Gaby shouted.

Fletch froze, a contrite expression hitting his face. "Aw, hell. Gaby, I didn't think to grab a condom."

"That's not the problem. I brought home a new condom to test. Do you mind?"

"Where are they?" Liam asked. "I'll get them."

"In the brown bag on the floor over there. Bring the lube as well. I'm trying a new flavor and want to see what you think."

Liam grabbed the bag she'd indicated and returned to the bed. "You want both of us to try the condom?"

"Please."

Fletch pulled out and went to grab a condom. Liam batted his hands away. "I'll put it on for you."

"You just want to fondle my cock," Fletch grumbled.

"Damn straight." Liam smiled, his heart lurching against his ribs as he unwrapped the condom and rolled it onto Fletch's dick. While this wasn't what he'd had in mind when he'd told Fletch he wanted to date Gaby, he couldn't be sorry at this turn of events. In fact, he didn't know why he'd never considered it before. No, not quite right. If it hadn't been for Fletch's forward thinking they'd still be fighting for Gaby's attention. Unable to help himself, he leaned close to kiss Fletch and gave Fletch's cock a furtive stroke at the same time.

Fletch didn't tense or back away. Instead, he moaned into Liam's mouth, a shudder racking his body. Gradually, Liam drew away to roll a condom onto his own cock. Fletch returned to Gaby, surging inside her with a seamless stroke.

Gaby's eyes slid to half-mast and a soft sigh emerged from her. Fletch started to move with steady strokes. Liam kneeled on the mattress at Gaby's side. He tapped his cock against her lips in a silent demand for her to open her mouth. When she did, heat surrounded him, the condom little barrier to his enjoyment.

"That's real good, Gaby. Your mouth feels great. Take more of me. Yeah, that's the way." He broke off on a groan when she applied suction—hot, intense suction that was like a bolt of lightning to his nuts.

Wanting to return the favor and heighten her pleasure, he leaned closer to flick his tongue over her nipple. Her moan was a vibration around his cock head. His belly muscles tensed when she lifted a hand to caress him, her fingers grasping his hip, biting into his flesh.

"That feel good, Liam? Gaby sure feels good on this end." Fletch continued his measured strokes and Liam started to do shallow thrusts in time with his friend. In. Out. In. Incredible warmth surrounding his dick. Good. So fuckin' good.

Fletch started to move faster, ramping up the pace. Liam's balls drew up, the assault of Gaby's mouth too much for him to hold back an instant longer. The heat exploded from him in the form of a climax that stole rational thought. He shuddered, drawing back when the lap of Gaby's tongue became too much for him.

His body hummed with residual satisfaction while he watched Fletch's face, contorted with pleasure. Liam removed the condom and tossed it aside. He kissed Gaby and, unable to resist, he leaned over to kiss Fletch too, messing with his rhythm.

"You close, Gaby?" Liam asked, grinning at Fletch.

"What about me?" he demanded.

"Gaby?" Liam's grin widened. No doubt there would be payback in his future.

"Yes...I need." She met Fletch's inward stroke with an upward one of her own.

Liam smirked at Fletch and slid his hand between their bodies, stroking a finger over her clit. She made a soft, yielding sound.

Fletch pulled back and started to hammer wildly into her. Liam moved his hand and watched Fletch's face. He sensed exactly what he was feeling, the boil of semen in his balls and every nerve ending snapping to attention as he savored the clinging fit of Gaby's pussy. Liam knew the moment Fletch climaxed and was mesmerized by the expression on his face. He rolled closer to Gaby and placed a hand on Fletch's back, reveling in the connection with the two people he loved most in the entire world.

"Aw hell," Fletch said after withdrawing. "The condom broke."

"Bother. Where's the clipboard?"

Liam leaned over to grab the clipboard and handed it to Gaby. She pulled the attached pen free and scribbled some notes.

"What happened to the wrapper?"

Fletch retrieved it from the floor and read out the code for her.

Liam shrugged. "The one I used was okay."

"I obviously have super sperm," Fletch drawled.

"No problem. That's the reason I'm on the Pill. How were the sensations?"

"Good for me," Liam said.

"Me too. No complaints."

"I might have to go up a fraction thicker with the latex." Gaby jotted another note before dropping the clipboard on the floor. "We didn't test the lube. You guys up for another go-round."

Liam exchanged a grin with Fletch. "Hell yeah."

"Bring it on," Fletch agreed.

Chapter Eleven

GABY'S LAB PHONE RANG a fraction after eleven the next morning. It was Alice requesting a meeting. "Do you want me to come now?"

"If you can spare the time. We've done the advertising mock-ups and we'd like your input."

Most of the board was present when Gaby walked into the boardroom. Loud shouts streamed through an open window and the oldies were doing their best to talk over the commotion.

Curiosity propelled Gaby to ask the question. "What's the racket about?"

James scowled at each of the board members in turn. "Somehow, the Children of Nature cult has learned about our new product."

Gaby stiffened. "They didn't find out about it from me."

Richard Morgan came stomping into the boardroom, newspapers clamped under his arm. "The *Sloan Gazette* has reinstated Ms. Knowall's gossip column."

"What?" James stretched out his hand. "Let me see."

Richard slapped the papers on top of the board table. "Hinekiri told me to bring a few papers." His grim voice and darting look at her made Gaby's insides twist. She remembered when Ms. Knowall ran her last column. For some reason she'd stopped her column as suddenly as she'd started writing it.

"I can't find my glasses." Katarina rifled through her bag with one hand and grabbed the last remaining paper with the other.

For a few frantic seconds the rustling of newsprint was the only sound in the room.

"Which page," Ben demanded finally.

"Page eleven," Katarina answered, peering closely at the page number.

"Gaby!" Gran said. "You're in the gossip column."

"But I haven't..." Oh, god. Surely there wasn't something about Liam and Rachel.

"Give me a paper," Alice said with a touch of impatience. "I'll read the item out loud." She folded the paper and scanned the first few lines before lifting her head to search out Gaby. "Oh dear." She made a *tsking* sound at the back of her throat. "'Sources close to me have informed us of Miss M and her untraditional living arrangement. Miss M, who works for Fancy Free, lives with two men and they don't have their own bedrooms, if you know what I mean. Another source has confirmed Miss M is the inventor of a new condom for Fancy Free. I wonder who she asks to help with testing.

"'And sticking to the Miss M theme, another source informs me one of her roommates is the father of a baby. Imagine this, readers—the man is denying everything. The mother, Miss S, is having a difficult time getting Mr. R to accept responsibility. He's had his fun and now he's denying everything. A case of like father, like son, me thinks.'"

Gaby listened to Alice with increasing horror. Someone knew. Someone had discovered she, Liam and Fletch were more than good friends. She drew a sharp breath when Alice read about Rachel's pregnancy. That wasn't fair. Now everyone would expect Liam to marry her and they weren't even positive he was the father. She scowled, aware of the clear speculation in the boardroom.

"Do you have anything you want to say, missy?" Joseph Craig asked in his gruff voice.

Katarina peered over the top of her reading glasses. "Is it true? That's what I want to know."

"I always liked Fletch and Liam, but both of them, Gaby?" Sam asked.

Gaby swallowed and remained silent. *Deny everything*, a voice screamed in her head. No one knew the truth. This was supposition.

Ben's shrill whistle cut through the silence, making Gaby flinch. "Your mother is going to have a cow."

"You don't have to sound so pleased about it," Alice said in a chiding manner.

Gran snorted. "Ben's right. She'll be gunning for you, Gaby."

"If she doesn't disown me first," Gaby said in a glum voice. Even though Ms. Knowall had used initials, the connection with Fancy Free would help everyone guess the identities of the supposedly guilty parties. Oh heck. No doubt most of Sloan's residents had read the scurrilous gossip already.

One thing was certain—Fletch and Liam could kiss goodbye any chance of winning the contract on the new subdivision.

Katarina reached for her coffee cup and frowned at the lack of contents. She set it back down with a clatter. "Do you have any comment?"

Deny everything. "I don't know anything about this." Gaby was proud she managed to meet the gaze of each of the oldies without a blush.

"I'll be back in a sec." James left the boardroom, his expression grim.

The chants of the cult members carried through the window. "Down with condoms. Condoms are bad. Population growth for Sloan. Down with condoms."

"That's a new one," James said, appearing back in the boardroom. "I didn't realize we were directly responsible for inhibiting population growth. I thought I might have an idea of the person who wrote this, but they're not responsible. They're in Australia."

A burst of babble and speculation rang out, pandemonium filling the boardroom.

"Maybe we could study the design boards?" Gaby wanted to run and hide. She wanted to ring Fletch and Liam to warn them about the gossip column. She did neither. "I'm working on a new design and I would like to get on with my experiments," she said, trying not to act defensive at the number of smirks leveled in her direction.

"Gaby's right," James said. "Besides, if she has more excellent designs up her sleeve, we want to encourage them."

"Hear, hear." Alice nodded emphatically. She switched on the projector screen and tapped several buttons on her laptop. "What do you think about this?"

It was perfect, a more polished print ad than the rough one Alice had shown Gaby earlier. The title was the same—*Christmas is Coming*. A picture of a Christmas tree and a couple exchanging a gift. The parcel bore Fancy Free's distinctive motif of the joined Fs. At the bottom of the ad, the words—*Give your lover the gift of pleasure*—were emblazoned.

"That's perfect." Gaby didn't have to pretend enthusiasm. "The vibrators are going to fly off the shelves."

"Along with the other gift packages Alice and I decided to market at the same time. We have condom and lube combos plus the main one of the vibrator. All of the packages will be wrapped in gold with red-and-green ribbon and we've decided to do a seasonal Vibrations condom in Christmas colors too."

"I like it," Gran said, and the other oldies agreed.

"That was easy," Alice said to James. "I think we're done."

Before any of the oldies had a chance to ask more noisy questions, Gaby stood and casually left the boardroom. She kept her steps slow and measured, despite every urge inside telling her to run.

"Gaby?" Alice followed her from the room.

"Yes?" The last thing she wanted to do was chat. She had to ring Fletch and Liam, warn them of possible fallout.

Then she'd screen her phone calls. She winced, imagining the blast she'd receive from her mother. How long could she dodge her calls before her mother decided to visit in person?

Alice strode down the passage to stand beside her. Sympathy shone in her eyes and she gave Gaby a swift hug.

"Don't worry about the gossip. Ignore everything. James and I understand what you're going through. If you need to talk or want someone to rant to you know where to find me."

"Will the gossip hurt sales?"

Alice grinned. "Hell no. The pre-gossip about Vibrations built expectation and buyers pounced the moment stock hit the shelves. James and I were trying to think of a way of dragging the Children of Nature cult out to protest and organize petitions because their demonstrations worked so well last time." Alice patted her arm. "You keep feeding the gossip mill and we'll all reap the rewards."

"You don't know my mother," Gaby said dryly.

"Don't worry. Everything will work out."

Gaby nodded but didn't believe it for an instant. Her mother and sister would probably disown her while Liam and Fletch would cop some flack too. How could everything be all right?

Back at the lab, Marc lifted his head from his microscope to scrutinize her. "What have you been up to? The phone has rung nonstop with people wanting to talk to you. I couldn't concentrate and took the bloody thing off the hook."

"My mother?"

"And your sister among others."

"Okay." A lie. Nothing was okay about this situation.

"Anything you want to tell me?"

"No." Marc would find out soon enough. "I have to make a phone call." Gaby plucked her cell phone from her pocket and left the lab, seeking somewhere private to make her call. Outside in the small rear garden the workers used for lunch and smoke breaks, she dialed Liam. His phone was busy. She tried Fletch next.

"Hi, sweetheart. What's up?" He listened while she told him everything.

"Fuck. Liam is with Rachel's father, delivering our bid."

"He wouldn't do anything stupid, would he?"

"Liam?"

"No, Robert Saunders."

Fletch paused. "He's not a hothead."

"This must be hitting close to home for Liam with his mother." Liam didn't like to talk about his mother, but she remembered the teasing he'd received at school. She might have been a few years younger, but even she'd been aware of the ridicule he'd faced at the hands of the other children.

"Don't worry. We'll circle the wagons. If anyone asks questions, deny everything. The gossip column is mere speculation. No one knows the truth apart from us."

"But what about your business? Won't this hurt you both?"

"It's true some of our clients are traditional and might believe the gossip, but we should be okay. We've built a solid reputation." Fletch chuckled. "Besides, you're gonna make lots of money at Fancy Free. I fancy being a kept man."

Gaby laughed as he'd meant her too. "A couple of male slaves would work well for me."

Fletch sobered. "Just as long as you don't let gossip scare you away, Gaby."

"No." A reply straight from the heart. She didn't know how or when this shift in her thoughts occurred but their relationship felt right. The three of them together didn't seem wrong or unnatural.

"Good. I'll get hold of Liam. Hang tight, sweetheart. Ignore the comments."

With a sigh, Gaby returned to the lab and put the phone back on the hook. The ringing started immediately.

"Fancy Free lab," Gaby said.

"You told me you had separate rooms," her mother shrieked down the line.

"What are you talking about?" Gaby played dumb. Much safer that way.

"The paper says you sleep in the same room."

"What paper? I have no idea what you're talking about. Look, Mum. I'm flat out. I'll talk to you later." Gaby ignored the squawk coming down the line and hung up on her mother.

By the time Gaby arrived home that night, exhaustion dogged her and her throat ached from denying the rumors floating around Sloan. Everyone she met during the course of the day expressed an opinion. The wink-wink nudge-nudge got to her after a while and it was a relief to enter the haven of their home and shed her work persona for a pair of jeans, a comfortable shirt and bare feet.

The light on the answer phone blinked insistently. Gaby grabbed a pen and pad and jabbed the message replay button. Her mother. Her sister. Her father. Gran. Rachel. Rachel's father.

Gaby's pen stilled at the harsh tone of his voice—so different from the affable man of the previous evening. The newspaper owner wanting an interview with her about the new Fancy Free products. Several hang-ups. The leader of the Children of Nature cult.

187

Color her complimented by the attention. In between the identified callers, several anonymous insults came from people calling them depraved, among other things. Fletch's mother had also called, along with his two brothers. Liam was probably glad of his lack of family at this stage, although Fletch's mother had included Liam in her terse message.

The tape was full. Gaby hit delete and turned off the answer phone. When the phone started to ring, she disconnected the plug at the wall.

What was wrong with everyone? It was her life and she'd live how she chose. No one should dictate behavior to her.

Gaby grabbed a bottle of wine from the fridge and poured herself a glass. It was her turn to cook dinner and she grabbed a chicken from the fridge, stuffing the cavity with herbs and a cut lemon before popping it in an oven bag. Once the oven heated, she placed the chicken inside and put on the timer. Glad of the mindless task of cooking, she peeled potatoes and prepared a salad.

Her cell phone chirped, indicating the arrival of a text. *Late home. Don't wait dinner for us.*

Gaby considered plonking herself in front of the telly. She tried to sit down but immediately shot to her feet again, unable to concentrate. She checked the time on the microwave clock and came to a decision. Once the chicken

188

was cooked, she'd go out.

In her bedroom, she exchanged her comfortable shirt for a formfitting one. The shirt hem stopped two inches short of the band of her low-slung jeans. Gaby pulled the band from her hair and dragged her fingers through the long locks, letting it swing around her shoulders in wild curls. A pair of strappy sandals with spike heels and a quick makeup refresh, topped with a bold red lippy, finished her preparations. Under no illusions, she knew this trip to the Cricket would be difficult. The messages on the answer phone told the story, but she refused to hide in shame. No, she wanted to enter the Cricket with head held high, her shoulders back in a show of pride. She cared for both Liam and Fletch and she liked the person she was when she spent time with them.

Their relationship was so new and untried. It wasn't fair for a gossip columnist to take something precious and judge them dirty and unnatural. If people—friends and neighbors and family—couldn't deal they had a problem, not her.

During the quick drive to the pub, she let her mind prod and worry at the problems she'd experienced with her latest developmental product. Soon the local council would put up Christmas decorations and festoon the street lamps with greenery and bright red candles. The big

Christmas tree would go up near the cafe, ready for the Christmas parade and Santa's arrival in Sloan.

The pub was busy for a Thursday night. She parked her car, grabbed her handbag and took a deep breath to steady the swirl of nerves in the pit of her stomach.

If anything, the gossip column had made her come to a decision. She wanted Fletch and Liam in her bed, both together and separately, whether they were testing Fancy Free products or not. She loved both men already and was rapidly falling *in* love with them. No matter what friends and family said or how they judged, she didn't intend to back away from a lifetime of possible happiness, not without exploring the potential.

Gaby pushed through the double doors leading into the Cricket. Live music from a local band poured from the right side of the large room and several couples were struttin' their stuff on the small dance floor. She scanned the crowd, smiling at the people she knew and ignoring the snubs from those who turned away. Oh yeah. Everyone read the *Sloan Gazette*.

At the bar, she slid onto a barstool and ordered a glass of sauvignon blanc before glancing around to see if people were still staring. The first person she noticed was Fletch's younger brother. He sauntered up to the bar and slung an arm around her shoulders.

"Hey, Gaby. How are you doing?" Craig asked. They'd gone to school together and had even dated casually a couple of times. With no romantic spark between them, they'd graduated to friends.

"I've had better days," she said. "You?"

"Fletch and Liam keep us busy. You want to come and sit with us? We're hanging out near the pool table. Grayson and Marie are crowing that no one can beat them. What do you say we whip their butts?"

"If you're sure."

Craig squeezed her shoulder in quick reassurance. "If my big bro is clever enough to catch you, I say he's smart."

"And what about Liam?"

Craig whistled softly. "It's true?"

"Your ears only. To anyone else I'm gonna deny everything."

A speculative glint entered his gaze then he grinned. "Two smart men. Only you could keep those two in line. I'm not judging. You're my friend."

"Other people have opinions."

"Fuck 'em." Craig waved at the bartender and ordered several drinks. "Want a top up?"

"Thanks." Gaby picked up several drinks and followed Craig over to the pool tables at the left side of the bar.

"Look who I found," Craig said.

Gaby realized she'd tensed and forced her shoulders to relax. Deny everything. She didn't owe anyone explanations, but she was aware of the wave of furtive whispers following her through the pub, the conjecture. The open disgust in some people, some of them supposedly her friends, hurt.

"Gaby," Marie said with a smile. She glanced past her to study the crowd. "Where are Liam and Fletch? They're usually half a step behind you."

Gaby wasn't blind to the intense interest in her reply, their avid attention waiting like a caged beast ready to spring and take her down. Marie's question was an innocent one—she hadn't meant to draw attention—it was there in the widening of her eyes and the horrified expression. She clapped her hand over her mouth.

Gaby laughed. "They're at work. We're roomies, not attached at the hip." She paused to take a sip of wine, pleased with her performance, the lack of tremor in her hand.

"Is Fletch dating anyone?" one of Marie's friends asked.

"I think he's been too busy at work," Gaby said, taking care with her answer because this question held a potential trap.

"It's true," Craig said. "We're doing a lot of overtime at present. You ready for a rematch? Gaby has agreed to play."

Although Craig's friends talked to her during the course of the evening, she was aware of the whispers behind her back, the rumors flying from mouth to ear. Gaby ignored them to concentrate on the pool game. She leaned over the table, eyed the corner pocket and struck the white cleanly. The ball dropped into the pocket.

"Great shot!" Craig said. "Do it again."

Laughing, Gaby sank the black and ended the game.

Craig whooped and drew her into a bear hug and pressed a noisy kiss to her cheek. Gaby drew back laughing, her merriment dying when she noticed a woman standing near Marie and the others.

Rachel.

Great. That was all she needed.

She let Craig guide her back to the table. He handed her glass to her and she accepted the wine with a smile.

"Excellent game," he said.

"Gaby is good at games," Rachel said in a loud voice. "She makes a game of stealing other women's men."

Gaby gasped. "I do not!"

"If it wasn't for you, Liam would accept me. He wouldn't throw me away like yesterday's trash and reject our baby." Her fingers curled around her glass so tightly Gaby feared it might not stand the strain. Gaby's attention went to the drink. If Rachel was pregnant, why the heck

SHELLEY MUNRO

was she drinking alcohol? Because call her stupid, but Rachel's drink didn't look like a soda.

Gaby backed up, not wanting to engage or encourage any more animosity. Rachel prowled after her, not giving her the chance to escape.

"You're ashamed," she said, a triumphant note in her voice. "And you should be."

A hand settled on Gaby's shoulder and she jumped in fright.

"Steady," Liam said in a low voice.

Rachel's features twisted, her eyes turning flat and hard. Determined. "Why are you doing this to me?" She tossed her drink in Gaby's face, burst into tears and fled, pushing her way through the crowd.

"Are you okay?" Liam asked, ignoring the interested bystanders to wipe off her face.

"I'm fine." Gaby scowled in the direction Rachel had disappeared.

"You should marry her," someone in the crowd said.

"Yeah, you can't have your fun and not accept the consequences," someone else muttered.

Fletch joined them and the mutters increased.

"It's sick," a woman said in a loud voice. "Against god's laws."

Another woman added her five cents to the

194

conversation. "You're a selfish woman, snapping up two good men instead of being happy with one."

"I'm going home to change out of these sticky clothes," Gaby said.

"Why did you come to the pub?" Liam demanded in a low voice. "You must have realized everyone would gossip and give you a hard time."

"This isn't the place," Fletch said. "Let's go." He wrapped his hand around her waist and propelled her from the pub. "Keys?"

Gaby pulled her keys from her handbag and handed them to him. He opened the passenger door and waited for her to get in before closing the door and heading around to the driver's side.

"I'm not an invalid."

"Humor me, okay? Liam and I've had a crap day. All I want to do is go home, have a shower and crawl into bed with both of you."

Gaby swallowed at the sheer need in his voice, the depth of feeling. He'd verbalized exactly what she craved.

When they arrived back at their house, Fletch parked her car. "Wait there."

"You don't have to act the gentleman for me."

"I want to look after you," he said, jumping out of her car before she could formulate a reply.

"You don't open the door for Liam."

"I would if he'd let me," Fletch said. "But we're keeping things low key in public." He hustled her out of the car before she asked more questions, but they littered her mind. So many questions and possible answers.

Liam unlocked the front door and stood aside for her and Fletch to enter. The door shut behind them and the tension ratcheted sharply upward. Not scary hostility but something right and natural.

"Let's get you out of this wet shirt," Fletch said.

"I'll turn on the shower. Rachel's aim was off and I'm sticky too." Liam brushed a kiss over her cheek and left them alone in the entranceway. Seconds later the water went on, reminding her of steady rain.

Fletch tugged her into the bathroom and bent to unfasten her shoes. He helped her balance while she kicked them out of the way. Standing again, he undid a couple of buttons and lifted the fitted shirt over her head then reached behind to unfasten her bra. "God, you're beautiful." He brushed his knuckles over the swell of one breast. "The only thing that's kept me going today is the knowledge I was coming home to spend time with you and Liam."

He pushed her jeans down, taking her tiny panties with them. She stepped out of the denim. "Into the shower with

Liam." He swatted her butt as he sent her on her way.

When she glanced back, she saw him watching her, lust on his face. She winked and waggled her butt, making him laugh. Smiling, she joined Liam who was already standing under the spray.

"Rough day?" She edged him away from the nearest showerhead and let the warm water pour over her chest to wash away the sticky drink.

"Rachel's father tore up our bid and he's spread the word. The work we'd lined up is drying up for one reason or another. We've received several cancellations."

"Can they do that?"

Liam dragged a hand through his hair and shrugged. "They've done it."

"Can you keep your crew on?"

"Not if we don't get any jobs." Fletch stripped rapidly. "Don't use all the hot water."

Gaby grabbed the soap and scrubbed it over Liam's back.

"Squish over," Fletch said, joining them in the wet area.

Liam cursed when his back hit the cold wall. "Damn, we need another shower head. I told you we should have put in three."

"Stop whining," Fletch said. "Get your butt moving into the bedroom and I'll warm you up."

Liam stilled. "Promise?"

"Things might have turned to shit at work but I don't intend to let vicious tongues kill the best thing in my life. You and Gaby belong here with me."

Liam pushed away from the wall, out of the reach of the water and grabbed a towel. "I thought you might have changed your mind."

"Not me." Fletch's gaze drifted from her to Liam, his usual humor absent. "I say we ignore the crap and ride out the storm. Another scandal will come along and people will forget about us."

"You think?" Gaby stepped out of the water and relaxed into Liam's embrace, allowing him to help her dry off.

Fletch turned off the water. "It'll take a while, especially with Rachel fanning the flames."

"I still say she's not carrying my baby," Liam said.

Gaby shrugged. "I vote we change the subject."

"I'll second that." Liam grabbed her right hand and dragged her from the bathroom toward Fletch's bedroom. He lifted her off her feet and tossed her onto the bed. He spread her legs and lowered his head to get busy. His warm tongue going down her slit brought a moan of delight.

Fletch sauntered into his room. "Now that's a sight to behold. Is there room for me?"

"Oh god." They intended to kill her with sex. Already,

she trembled on the cusp of orgasm, climbing fast with a few flicks of Liam's tongue.

"I think she likes the idea," Fletch said, the edge of amusement in his husky voice. "But first..." He kissed Liam. Not a gentle kiss or an easy one he typically bestowed on her. This was more aggressive, laced with passion. Promise.

Gaby braced on her elbows, watching them through narrowed eyes. "I've said it before and it bears repeating. It makes me incredibly hot to see the two of you kiss."

The two men parted, both turning to stare at her.

"It really does?" Liam asked.

"Oh yeah."

"I like watching you and Fletch too," Liam said, his expression telling Gaby the admission surprised him.

Fletch chuckled, gave Liam another swift kiss before lowering his head to lick around her clit. "Pretty," he said, the puff of air from his words sending a shudder of decadent warmth through her.

Never in her wildest dreams had she considered a relationship so much out of the norm. Another shudder went through her as she considered the coming confrontation with her mother. She'd probably disown her. Luckily her father was a bit more progressive, although this situation might throw him.

Then Liam and Fletch drove her concerns away, the flicker of their tongues over her labia and sly forays across her clit shoving her on edge. Her hands gripped the duvet cover, creasing the cotton as she attempted to stave off the waiting leap into pleasure. They petted her, licked her and occasionally paused to kiss each other.

"Don't hold back, love," Liam said.

Fletch stroked her hip with his callused fingers. "Yeah, we have more in us."

Their encouragement sent her flying hard and fast. A small scream erupted from her, the pulse of her pussy going on for long moments.

"I think she liked that," Liam said.

"Can you take both of us?" Fletch asked, already reaching for the lube.

"Yes." If there was one thing she needed tonight it was togetherness and reinforcing the invisible strands of their relationship. "We're not going to let close-minded people ruin this for us."

"I'm in for the long haul," Fletch said instantly.

Liam tugged on her nipples hard, the streak of pain jolting her. "Why would you think otherwise? If we lose jobs, things might be a bit tough financially, but this is one thing I'm positive about. I've never had people in my life like you and Fletch. We're family. The two of you fill the empty spaces inside me." He shut his mouth with a snap of teeth and a faint tide of color seeped into his face, highlighting his gorgeous blue eyes.

Gaby went soft inside. "That's the way I feel. Kiss me, Liam."

He moved up the bed, taking her in his arms. She tasted her juices on his mouth when their lips met. Fletch stretched out beside her, his rough fingers exquisitely gentle as he stroked one breast. He lowered his head and took her nipple into his mouth, sucking almost painfully hard. Gaby relaxed under the attention. This had happened so quickly between them, but she couldn't be sorry, despite the storm of gossip and disapproval.

Fletch moved away and opened the bottle of lube. He turned her onto her side, rearranging her body to his satisfaction. She flinched at the coldness of the lube when he massaged it over her pucker. He stretched her carefully. First one finger. Once she took him comfortably, he added another.

"Put the condom on for me, Liam?" There was a dare in his voice, and Gaby felt him tense a fraction, as if he thought Liam might balk at the suggestion, despite performing the service for him before.

Liam opened the nightstand drawer and pulled out a Fancy Free condom, one of the experimental ones she'd asked them to test for her. He opened the plain packet and moved down the bed.

"Not ready for a condom," Liam said.

"What do you mean?" Fletch demanded. "I—" He broke off with a strangled groan when Liam took his cock into his mouth. Gaby grinned at his shock, and the way it rapidly slackened into a haze of pleasure when Liam sucked and licked him. He obviously reached all the good points, judging by Fletch's expression. "Fuck, not too much. I want to come inside Gaby with our cocks touching, with the three of us together."

Liam pulled off his cock with a loud pop. "That's better." Satisfaction echoed in his face. With competent moves, he rolled the latex down Fletch's length. "Anything else?"

"Not at present," Fletch said, his eyes narrowing when Gaby and Liam laughed at him. "You'll keep," he added in warning. They laughed harder, and finally he huffed and moved behind her. He pressed against her pucker, pushing in carefully, pressing forward and withdrawing until she took him easily. Once he was fully embedded, he waited while Liam worked into Gaby's pussy.

"I don't think I'm ever gonna get tired of the connection I feel when we're together like this," Gaby said, her tone dreamy. "It feels good. Right. I love you guys."

"Glad to hear it," Fletch said, shuddering at the drag of Liam's cock when he withdrew from her pussy, unhurried as if they had all the time in the world.

Liam pushed back inside, stopping when he was balls-deep. "We feel the same way."

"You ready for us to start moving in earnest?" Fletch asked.

"Please," she whispered. Instead of closing her eyes as she normally did, she watched Liam's face. The pleasure she saw in him rippled over her, both inside and out. Her men did good work together. Like a well-oiled machine, they pushed her higher and higher.

"Damn. Can't hold on any longer," Fletch said, his next thrust erratic.

Liam reached down to finger her slippery clit, the insistent brush of his finger sending her soaring. A spasm went through her pussy, the hard clench around a cock bringing satisfaction. Like a ripple effect, the pleasure shot through them all until they collapsed in a sweaty heap.

After a quick cleanup, they cuddled with her in the middle.

"Do we need to make a plan?" Liam asked.

"As long as we stick together and refuse to talk, we should be okay," Fletch said.

"What about your family? Gaby's family?"

"My mother and sister have already left messages." Gaby couldn't restrain her scowl. She tried so hard with them, but she'd concluded that nothing she did would ever gain their approval. They were too different in their beliefs. "Gran and everyone at work will support me. I know that without even thinking about it."

"My family could go either way," Fletch said, doubtfully. "I don't know."

"You love your family. Hell, I love your family because they've treated me like a son ever since the time I came home from school with you," Liam said.

"I can't pretend a rejection won't hurt, but I love you guys, both of you. You're my family," Fletch said.

Liam let out a heavy sigh. "The next few weeks will tell."

"What I don't understand is how the paper found out. I haven't told anyone." Gaby's brow creased. "No wait. I talked to Gran about testing the sex toys with you both, but she's the only person I've discussed it with. She wouldn't tattle."

"We haven't discussed our changed relationship with anyone apart from each other," Liam said, and Fletch nodded agreement.

"I suppose someone might've guessed." Gaby scowled again. "Unless we have a peeping Tom spying on us and peeking through our windows."

"I say we behave normally and try to ignore the inevitable comments," Fletch said.

"That's all we can do," Liam agreed.

"What about Rachel?"

"I've made it clear I won't marry her. I'll ask for DNA tests once the baby's born and if it's mine, I'll offer financial support. I don't love her. It was sex, dammit, and I made it clear to her at the time. She knew the score."

"That's a bit brutal," Fletch said.

"You think I should marry her?"

"Hell no. I just mean she's probably scared," Fletch said. "I sure as hell wouldn't marry her either. She's a flake."

"I think she's putting on an act," Gaby said. "There was something calculated about her display tonight. She went out of her way to make everyone sympathetic toward her."

"You don't think she's pregnant?" Liam asked.

"No, I think she's pregnant. It's too easy to disprove. She either knows the real father will reject her or knows her family don't approve of him. She's trying to land a husband her father approves of."

"You didn't hear him today," Liam said drily. "He was pissed about me rejecting his daughter, and the idea of the three of us together horrified him. He said it was against everything the church taught."

"You forgot the bit about ruining us," Fletch muttered.

"Don't worry," Gaby said. "He can't do that. Pray for another scandal and we'll be yesterday's news soon enough."

Chapter Twelve

Late November

FLETCH AND LIAM WERE working in the garden when Gaby arrived home. Both bare-chested, their torsos gleaming in the late-afternoon sun. A sight to behold. She sighed in appreciation.

"Very sexy," she purred.

"We've been here most of the day," Liam said tersely.

Gaby grimaced. "Oh. I'm sorry."

Fletch draped a sweaty arm around Liam's tense body and gave him a quick hug. "Don't be sorry, sweetheart. It's not your fault."

Liam finally relaxed a fraction, sagging into Fletch's embrace. "We had to lay off the rest of the staff."

"Did you finish putting up the last of the hay sheds?"

"Yep, all done," Fletch said. "It's official. We don't have any work because Rachel's father has blackballed us."

"James and Alice invited us to a barbecue tonight. You

guys want to go?"

Her two men exchanged a quick glance.

"Sure," Fletch said.

"We could do with some tension release first," Liam suggested slyly.

The garden was private, their closest neighbor unable to see their house let alone the garden. Gaby sank to her knees in front of Liam and dragged down his shorts.

"Ooh, I like the way she thinks." Fletch looked on with interest as she guided Liam's cock into her mouth and took him deep. His flavor burst over her, musky, a little sweaty and all male.

Liam groaned, his hands coming down to hold her head. Unable to help himself, he started to thrust. She breathed through her nose, swallowing to control her gag reflex while her fingers stroked his balls. When she withdrew, her tongue snaked over his tip and around to tease the acutely sensitive part below. She glanced up to catch Fletch's gaze and he grinned. She watched him finger Liam's nipple before twisting it. During the last month they'd learned a lot about their likes and dislikes. Liam liked this and they were happy to oblige. Fletch kissed Liam, his fingers still busy. It was working. A rapid stream of pre-come filled her mouth and his balls drew up tight beneath his cock.

Fletch pinched Liam's nipple again and a jolt went

through Liam. She sucked hard and he started to come, shooting down her throat as she swallowed him down. When he'd finished she gradually eased up, licking him clean before pulling back.

"Is that better?" she asked.

"Only if you're Liam," Fletch complained.

Gaby laughed, and she rose to her feet, flashing a sly wink at Liam. Seconds later they attacked Fletch together. He didn't stand a chance. Not that he put up much of a fight.

THEY ARRIVED LATE TO the barbecue. When they walked around the back into James and Alice's garden, the area was full of laughing groups of friends and family. Fletch and Liam had been to a couple of barbecues with her before and knew everyone. Along with most of the board members and their spouses, Marc was present with a woman she didn't know. Luke Morgan, Richard's son and James' friend, was there with his wife Janaya. Richard's wife Hinekiri stood talking to Gran and a small black-and-white dog with spots ran from group to group seeking attention. The dog barked when she saw them and trotted toward them. Gaby smiled because she'd met Killer before.

Killer made a beeline for Fletch and rubbed against him before flopping to the ground and turning over to get her belly scratched. She barked the entire time, and Luke and Janaya laughed while Richard let out a disgusted snort.

"She likes you, Fletch," Luke said.

Gaby shook her head and grinned. "I've never known a dog to bark so much."

"Killer is very talkative. You could say she has an opinion about everything." Janaya smirked at her husband. "She's part of the family. We wouldn't be without her."

"But we'd let you borrow her anytime," Luke said.

Killer barked several times and moved on to seek attention from Liam.

Gaby relaxed when no one mentioned the rumors. Public outings were rare these days. With the continuing gossip, the three of them still featured in the *Sloan Gazette* gossip column on a regular basis.

James brought them drinks.

"I'd like to propose a toast," Alice said. "To Marc and Gaby our wonderful designers. Without them we'd be a very ordinary company. Instead our pre-Christmas orders are booming. It's shaping up to be a record year for us. So, to Marc and Gaby."

"To Marc and Gaby," everyone said.

After that, the conversation moved on to more general

things.

"The three of you are still making the gossip column," James said.

"We keep hoping something else will grab the headlines from us," Fletch said.

"We need another UFO sighting," Hinekiri chirped.

"No, we do not," Luke retorted. "The last time there was a sighting the police phone went all day and night for a week. I do not need more weeks of bedlam."

"I agree," Richard said. "The Sloan police department doesn't need that sort of excitement."

"The Sloan Ladies Division would welcome the money-making opportunity." Hinekiri winked. "One can only do so much knitting."

"God forbid," Luke muttered, rolling his eyes.

Liam and Fletch gravitated toward James and Luke.

Luke acknowledged them with a jerk of his chin. "The grapevine says Rachel's father blackballed you."

"Yeah. He'll be gloating tomorrow when it becomes public knowledge we let the last of our workers go. We can't afford to pay them," Liam said.

"Why don't you branch into furniture or something similar until things improve?" James said. "Or try making wooden trains or toys for the Christmas market. I remember the stuff you made at school workshop. You're both good."

"You could sell them at the farmers' market in Clevedon," Luke suggested. "Cut out the middleman."

"That's not a bad idea," Liam said slowly.

Fletch nodded, his expression distant as if he were thinking hard. "We have a load of timber and shorter off-cuts we kept, hoping to use them on another job. If we can sell a few things, it'll pay the bills."

"Robert Saunders always was an ass. Remember when Rachel accused Luke of chopping off her pigtails when we were at primary school?" James prodded the sausages and turned several of them. The scent of cooking meat filled the air. "Luke, hand me those vegetables, will you? I think everything else is almost cooked."

"I still remember the fuss. She always was a bit of a sneak. I saw her cut them off," Luke said.

Liam's mouth dropped open. "Why did she do that?"

"She wanted one of the short, trendy cuts her friends were getting, but her father wouldn't let her cut her hair. He likes women to wear their hair long."

Fletch glanced at Liam and laughed when his lover winked at him. "So shoot me, I'm partial to long hair too."

"I could've done without knowing that." James flipped off the burners apart from the one under the vegetables.

"I take it some of Ms. Knowall's columns have an

element of truth?" Luke handed his friend a plate for the sausages and steak.

"No comment," Fletch said.

"The no-comment thing worked real well for me," James said.

"It's something to do with Fancy Free." Luke cast a sly glance at his father. "Talking about sex and sex-related items must relocate the blood south. Nothing left to help the brain process. Makes you behave without thinking first."

"We don't work there," Liam pointed out.

"Gaby does," Luke countered.

"Gaby is a gifted designer." Fletch stole a glance at Liam.

Liam couldn't restrain his smug grin. Gaby bore all sorts of gifts—something to keep between him and Fletch. Despite the problems at work and the fact most of their family members weren't speaking to them, the last six weeks had been the happiest of his life.

"Your smirk tells me we want details," James said. "But we're damn pleased Gaby works for us. We couldn't do without her and Marc, especially after Rodney decided to stay in Spain."

Liam glanced over at Gaby to find her deep in discussion with Marc and his lady. To his relief, Gaby's body language said friend and nothing more.

"Does anyone know Ms. Knowall's identity?" Richard asked.

"It was my mother for a while," James said. "She's been visiting the grandchildren on the Gold Coast. Somehow I don't see her sending a column from Australia."

"The *Gazette* has two part-time reporters plus the owner," Fletch said. "We've kept an eye on them. It must be someone else."

"Has anyone considered Gaby's sister? Doesn't she fill in there sometimes? Isn't she friendly with one of the reporters?" Luke mused. "I've seen them have lunch together in the cafe."

"Hell," Fletch said. "Would Elsa do that to Gaby?"

"She's a jealous cat," Liam said. "I wouldn't put anything past her. I rebuffed an advance from her a few years ago before she married. She hasn't spoken to me since."

"No loss." James flipped a skewer of vegetables. "The vegetables are cooked." He transferred them to a plate and handed it to Luke.

Liam and Fletch grabbed a plate of meat each and the men joined the women.

Almost three hours later, they said their goodbyes. In the car, during the drive back to the house, Liam brought up the subject of Gaby's sister.

"Is it possible Elsa would know about us? I mean before the story hit?"

Gaby frowned. "Gran and I discussed testing sex toys and condoms when I went to my nephew's birthday party. We were alone, but it's possible Elsa eavesdropped."

"Or it's possible whoever wrote the column knew the three of us lived in the same house and took a calculated guess," Fletch said.

"Next time I see her, I'll ask her straight out." Gaby shrugged helplessly. "Not that it matters now. The damage is done. Learning the identity of the culprit won't change a thing."

Shopping for groceries was a pain in the butt. Normally she dragged one or both of the guys with her, but they were busy working on making stock to sell at their first farmers' market.

Gaby pushed the trolley down the supermarket aisles, mentally crossing items off her list and humming to the Christmas carols. Unable to resist she threw in a pack of candy canes to decorate their Christmas tree. She saw lots of women she'd gone to school with and many others she knew, but most of the women ignored her. The flurry of whispers that followed her was like background static on the sound system.

She rounded the corner and came face-to-face with her mother.

Gaby pasted a pleasant expression on her face. "Hi, Mum."

Her mother pushed her trolley past, sticking her nose in the air and ignoring her totally. Two women standing by the Christmas hams witnessed the snub and sniggered.

"Hussy," someone spat as she wheeled her trolley past the bread aisle. Gaby ignored the insult and tossed two loaves of wholegrain bread into the trolley. Maybe she should brand S for scarlet woman on her forehead or shave her hair or something. Honestly, she'd expected flak from her mother and sister, but this backlash and pettiness—never.

Sighing, she consulted her list and wheeled her trolley to the checkout. The teenage girl on the register stared but at least she didn't refuse to serve her. She'd suffered that indignity the previous week.

Outside, Gaby wheeled her trolley to the far end of the parking lot, past the bins of rubbish and food scraps waiting for collection by a local farmer. She unloaded the groceries into the car and wheeled her trolley to the collection point. She caught a flash of white from the corner of her eye and glanced up to find four cult members surrounding her. They held a placard each.

"You need to stop working at Fancy Free," one shouted.

"You're a fallen woman," another said. "A bad influence. You should encourage the birth of children."

"Birth control is bad," a third hollered, waving her placard.

Gaby's brows rose. She glanced at the fourth woman. "Do you have anything to add?"

"Yes, don't you think it's selfish to keep two men to yourself? One man. One woman!"

"Oh brother." Gaby rolled her eyes, a surge of anger zapping her. Fletch and Liam belonged to her and she belonged to them. No sharing allowed. "Excuse me." When the women didn't move, she pushed between two and tugged open the driver's door.

The women hoisted their placards and started marching around her car, shouting anti-condom slogans at the top of their voices.

Gaby started up her car and eased off the handbrake but the women stood their ground, blocking her way. Frustrated tears filled her eyes. It had been a hellish day all round. She'd burned her hand on hot latex while she was pouring a sample and the spot still throbbed like hell. She'd suffered through whispers and snubs when she'd ventured to the café for lunch with Alice and now this. She pressed on the horn but the women continued their chanting and obstinately blocked her departure.

She kept inching her car forward and suddenly one of the women fell in front of her vehicle with an ear-piercing shriek. Alarmed, she slammed on the brakes. She switched off the ignition and leaped out of her car. "Is she okay?"

"Call the cops," one of the cult women screamed. "She ran my friend down on purpose."

"Gaby Montgomery. I should've guessed," a mocking feminine voice came from behind her. "Not only do you steal boyfriends but you run down innocent bystanders. Call the cops. I'm a witness. I saw the entire incident."

"I did not run her down," Gaby snapped, turning to glare at Rachel. Her eyes narrowed on Rachel's belly, her brows drawing together in shock. That was an awful big baby bump if her dates were correct and Liam was the father.

A crowd gathered around Gaby and her car. The cult lady continued to screech and moan while her cohorts made enough din to prod the beginnings of her headache into full bloom.

"Stone her. Run her out of town!"

Gaby didn't see who made the comment, but they were stomping on her last nerve. "Stand out of my way so I can leave and get out of your sight. I wouldn't want to offend you for longer than necessary."

"You can't leave the scene of the crime," a man shouted. "You ran her down."

A gasp of shock emerged from Gaby. This wasn't a crime scene, not unless they counted the felony of narrow minds and gossiping old biddies. "I haven't done anything wrong."

Without warning, a tomato flew through the air, hitting her square in the chest. On the verge of over-ripeness, the tomato exploded on impact, squirting smelly juice over her black and white dress. Silence descended on the car park until someone snickered, breaking the hush.

"The perfect punishment," someone cried. "Pelt the scarlet woman with rotten tomatoes."

Horrified, Gaby tried to climb back inside her car but rough hands halted her escape.

The tomatoes she'd glimpsed earlier pelted her from myriad directions, the crowd roaring for her blood. She spied Rachel and two of her friends chortling in delight then lost sight of them as the crowd closed around her, roaring insults and flinging tomatoes.

Only the whine of a police siren halted the tomato throwing. Slowly, Gaby let her protective hands fall from her face. A tomato hit her face so hard, she saw stars.

Clutching her head, she slumped against her car.

The siren ceased. Thank goodness. Gaby concentrated on breathing, wincing when the cult woman started caterwauling again.

"What's going on here?" Luke's hard voice stopped the woman short.

The crowd started talking at once.

"She ran over a woman and tried to leave without rendering assistance."

"She's a criminal."

"Arrest that woman."

Footsteps stalked past her, but Gaby didn't open her eyes to look up. Instead she concentrated on holding her emotions together. She refused to fall apart and give the crowd the satisfaction of knowing they'd broken her.

A groan came from the front of her vehicle along with a masculine murmur. Another police car arrived and the crowd started to disperse.

"Gaby, you're bleeding," Richard Morgan said.

Gaby lifted her head, focusing with difficulty. "It's rotten tomato. I wouldn't come any closer if I were you."

"What happened?"

"The women from the cult surrounded my car when I tried to leave. One fell down."

"That's a lie. She ran over my friend. She's injured her

back and can't move."

Gaby couldn't believe these people. The woman was twisting the truth. "I—"

"I insist you charge her with attempted murder," one of the cult women said.

"Hear! Hear!" another woman agreed.

An ambulance arrived and two medical staff checked the woman before placing her in a stretcher, loading her up and driving away.

Unbelievable. She was positive she hadn't touched the woman with her car, not that anyone wanted to accept her version of events.

"You'd better come down to the station," Luke said.

"But—"

"He's arresting her," one of the women cried.

"About time," someone else said, satisfaction ringing through her tone.

Stony faced, Gaby glared at Luke. "What about my groceries? There are perishables in there."

Richard's expression held concern. "Go with Luke, Gaby. I'll get one of the constables to drive your car home. Are Fletch and Liam there?"

"Yes." Gaby squeezed her eyes shut for an instant, fighting the sting of tears. She would *not* give anyone the satisfaction of crying in public. "Tell them to unpack the groceries. I'll see them at home."

Richard frowned. "Don't you want them to come and collect you?"

"No." She'd lose her struggle to keep herself together if she let them collect her.

Richard exchanged a glance with his son and gave a curt nod. "I'll make sure your car and groceries get home."

Luke took her arm and escorted her to his car. He opened the rear door and waited until she was inside before closing the door. The last humiliation. She sucked in a deep breath and focused on the process. *In. Out.* As they drove out of the parking lot she caught a glimpse of Rachel standing outside the supermarket building, a toothy smirk on her face and, for the first time in her life, Gaby wanted to commit murder.

Chapter Thirteen

GABY MAINTAINED A STONY silence while Luke escorted her through the front entrance of the Sloan police station.

A local farmer was present, making a report about damage to his fences by the local high school students. With exams almost over and the Christmas holidays in sight, the students were starting to get up to pranks. The farmer's exasperated voice rose in anger and he started to harangue the constable attending to him.

"In here," Luke said, directing her into a room with a battered desk and two chairs. "Hell, you stink. My car will never smell the same."

Hurt sliced through Gaby, sending her a step closer to tears. "Being pelted with tomatoes wasn't my idea of a fun time."

"You're gonna have a black eye," Luke said, inspecting her more closely.

"Figures."

"Do you want to risk a cup of our coffee?"

"Sure. Make it black with one sugar." Gaby dropped onto one of the available chairs and slumped, holding her head in her hands once Luke departed. Alone, she cataloged her aches and pains. A nagging headache still gripped her while her eye and the entire right side of her face throbbed in concert. To top it off, her dress bore big splotches of stinky red tomato juice. Ruined. Even if she could get out the stains, the idea of wearing the dress again, with the associated memories, didn't seem likely.

"Here you go." Luke slid a mug across the table toward her.

Grateful for something to concentrate on, she cupped the mug in her hands. The warmth of the chunky china seeped into her palms, doing nothing to dispel the physical lethargy that had crept into her since she'd taken a seat. She was so tired of this, of being unable to appear in public without worrying about the reactions of people she met during the course of her outing. She was sick of the snubs, the catty comments. She was just plain tired.

"Tell me what happened," Luke said.

"I've told you." Frustration laced her response.

"Tell me again, right from the start."

With an exasperated sigh, Gaby recapped her visit to

the supermarket, leaving not one boring detail out. Luke jotted notes as she spoke. When she'd finished, he leaned back in his chair, tapping his pen against one muscled thigh.

"That's not what the witnesses I spoke to said."

"Are you implying I'm a liar?"

Luke straightened, studying her through narrowed eyes. "Of course not. All I'm saying is the eyewitness reports appear to differ from what you've told me."

"Fine," she gritted out. "Charge me. Lock me up. Do whatever you have to do."

Someone tapped on the door. "Come in," Luke said, still studying her closely.

Richard opened the door. "There's a phone call for you."

"Can't it wait?"

"It's an eyewitness. The supermarket situation."

Gaby's mouth twisted. Oh yeah. She'd created a situation all right. Her life was one big situation and, frankly, she couldn't take much more.

Luke left and Richard joined her in the room. Richard screwed up his nose. "It honks in here. Maybe I'll leave the door open."

"I don't need watching."

"Of course you don't," Richard said, setting his weight

on the chair. "Hinekiri liked your sex toy. I think she's getting Janaya one for Christmas."

Gaby appreciated his attempt to initiate a normal conversation, not that sex toys were normal. Richard was a good man as was his son Luke. The trouble was the only witnesses were the cult women, and they were lying through their teeth.

Luke arrived back. "Who served you in the supermarket?"

"A young girl. She looked like one of the Proctors."

Luke nodded. "She said she was on a break after she served you. She went outside to have a cigarette and saw everything. Evidently you didn't hit the woman with your car. She took a dive."

Gaby exhaled. "Are you taking her word for it?"

"She had no reason to lie. She also said Rachel was the first to fire a tomato and the rest of the crowd followed suit."

"Doesn't surprise me. She's a bitch."

"Do you want to press charges?"

"No."

Luke frowned. "Alice told Janaya you're getting hassled every time you go out in public."

"Yeah. It'll get old soon."

"I'll give you a ride home now." He fished his keys out

of his uniform pocket and waited for her to stand before ushering her out. He paused and turned back. "Dad, tell Hinekiri it's time to do a drive-by. Probably more than one."

Richard chuckled. "I'll pass on the message. See you and Janaya for dinner later on. See ya tomorrow at the meeting, Gaby."

"Sure."

"We'll go out the back door," Luke said.

Gaby hopped in the front this time and wound down the window to get rid of the worst of the smell. "You'll have to hose out your car."

"It's seen worse."

The ten-minute drive home didn't take long and soon Luke pulled up outside the house.

"What happens if the cult lady wants to press charges?"

"I'll speak to the medical staff and obtain a report on her injuries. Along with the witness you should be right."

"Thanks, Luke. I'm sorry about the stench in your car."

"Don't worry about it."

Gaby climbed out of the car and waved him goodbye. When the police car drove from sight, her shoulders slumped. She swallowed, her throat suddenly tight with a lump of emotion. All she wanted was to shower and go to bed, preferably alone.

Fletch and Liam stood in the kitchen, both freshly showered, judging by their damp hair. Liam stirred something on the stovetop while Fletch was busy chopping vegetables.

Fletch sighted her first. He set down his knife with a thump. "Fuck, is that blood? Do you need a doctor?" He strode around the countertop and came to an appalled stop. "What is that smell? What the hell happened to you? I thought you were with Luke."

"It's rotten tomatoes."

"What happened?" Liam asked.

Her throat constricted and the tears she'd managed to hold at bay, swamped her eyes. "The modern version of being stoned," she said, her voice cracking.

Fletch cursed while Liam went to take her into his arms.

She held up her hands. "No, I'm going to have a shower."

"Take your time," Fletch said.

Liam went back to his pot. "Dinner will keep."

"I'm not hungry." Her voice caught, a dull, empty sensation gnawing at her. A tear splashed onto the floor at her feet. Now that she'd started crying she couldn't stop. Gaby turned and fled, unable to hold herself together a moment longer.

"Gaby, wait," Fletch said.

Liam hauled on his arm, stopping him from following her. "Give her some time. She obviously wants to be alone right now."

"But what the hell happened? Richard didn't hint at anything wrong when he dropped off the car. I thought it was strange him bringing the car..." He trailed off at a loss. "What should we do?"

"Give Gaby some time. She's not sleeping well either. Her tossing and turning kept me awake last night."

Fletch went back to chopping vegetables but his mind dwelled on Gaby. "I love her. I can't lose her." He glanced up to catch an expression of panic on Liam's face. "I love you too. Goes without saying, numbskull. All I'm saying is Gaby looks at the end of her tether. We need to do something."

Liam turned off the gas on the element and reached for his cell phone. He hit speed dial. "Luke, it's Liam."

Fletch listened in approval as Liam grilled Luke. A few minutes later he hung up. "The cult women caused problems. A crowd gathered and Rachel incited the tomato throwing. Evidently it's not the first situation in town. Some of the women are being real bitches."

"Gaby should have told us. We have to stop this. It's not right."

"Rachel is at the root of a lot of our problems."

Fletch cursed. "Her old man isn't doing such a bad job either."

"But we're riding the storm out by working from home. Gaby doesn't have the same luxury because she works in town and has to face the public more than we do."

"How do we fix this mess?"

"Time to have this out with Rachel and her father. At the least we need to get them to back off Gaby. They're not being fair. It's me they're pissed at."

"Tomorrow?"

"It's a date."

Fletch chuckled. "I can think of better places to go for a date."

The water switched off in the bathroom.

"Give her more time," Liam suggested. "We'll take her something to eat a bit later."

SHE COULDN'T STOP CRYING. Tears streamed down her face as she stepped from the shower. A shiver sped down her body, a rash of chill bumps springing to life on her arms and legs. Sniffing, she blotted the water from her hair and wound a towel around her head like a turban. With a second towel, she rubbed her body dry.

Now tomato-free, the fatigue struck her worse than before. A yawn slipped free, her entire body aching. Her head still thumped and the nagging throb at her eye continued unabated. She peered at her eye in the mirror. Already black, it would look even worse tomorrow. She dug through the bathroom cupboard, found a packet of painkillers and took two tablets with a glass of water. After removing the towel around her head, she gingerly combed her hair. She wrapped the other towel around her body and left the bathroom.

The two men were still in the kitchen. She could hear a masculine hum of voices and smell the enticing aroma of spaghetti sauce. Wincing at a nasty jolt of pain at her temple, she shuffled down the passage, hesitating outside Fletch's bedroom. Gritting her teeth, she kept walking and turned into the bedroom she'd claimed as her own but hadn't used, except as a dressing room, for weeks. The door shut with a solid clunk after her. She drew the curtains, dropped the towel and crawled between the musty sheets, seeking oblivion in slumber.

Sleep didn't occur.

She tossed and turned, unable to find a comfortable spot. Pain embraced her skull like a lover, settling in for the duration. And her thoughts... Her thoughts chased round and round like the puppy she'd had as a child. She loved Fletch. She loved Liam.

It was that simple and that complicated.

There was no choosing one over the other because in her mind they came together. Fletch with his cocky, sometimes brash manner and great smile balanced Liam's quieter, more contemplative way. Physically they both attracted her, made her heart go pitter-patter.

But none of that was enough.

Love didn't make the world go round. Instead, the presence of love made her life messy and complicated.

A fresh batch of tears filled her eyes and this time a sob broke free. She couldn't do this anymore. The only people who spoke with her were her workmates. Everyone else treated her like a leper when all she'd done was follow her heart.

Gaby pushed back the covers and found a cotton dressing gown in her wardrobe. She walked down the passage, heading for the kitchen, feeling a bit like a condemned man.

Liam noticed her first. His lips curled in a gentle smile, taking his handsome face from serious to stunning. "Are you ready for something to eat?"

"No." She sniffed, wishing she'd taken the time to grab a hanky. "I'm not hungry."

"Sweetheart, you need to eat." Fletch grasped her hand and directed her to the table. He pulled out a chair and seated her.

Their care and concern brought more tears.

They reached her side in seconds. Fletch crouched at her feet, looking up at her while Liam rubbed her shoulders.

Another sob broke free. "I can't do this. I can't be with you anymore."

Fletch and Liam exchanged a quick glance before turning their full attention back on her. Liam pulled a couple of tissues from a box on the counter and handed them to her.

"Can't do what, sweetheart?" Fletch asked.

"I thought I could be with you both, but it's too...too hard." Unable to meet either of their gazes, she bowed her head and stared at her clenched hands until the rapid fall of tears shrouded her view. She blotted her eyes, but the tissues rapidly became a damp, sodden mess.

"Gaby, what's too hard?" Liam asked.

"I can't take the insults, the rude remarks." A shudder went through her, and she swallowed, attempting to force the lump in her throat away. It didn't work. The lump returned immediately. "The...the tomato throwing," she croaked. "I'm going to move out."

"Move out?" Liam's hand tightened on her shoulder

and she winced. He immediately removed his hand and started to pace.

"Wait a minute," Fletch said. "You can't let other people drive you away."

"You don't know what it's like. The constant snide remarks. The dirty innuendoes."

"But we're good together," Fletch said, a trace of urgency in his voice.

Gaby swiped a hand over her eyes. "It's not enough."

"We love you," Liam said. "Doesn't our love count for anything?"

Her resolve softened for an instant. She loved them too. Perhaps she always had. Their love was the one thing in this sorry mess that kept her going. "Sometimes love isn't enough."

"Where do you want to go?" Liam asked in a hard voice.

She flinched, his abruptness lashing like a whip. God, why did this have to hurt so much? Misery weighed her down and she felt alone, so alone. "I'll go to Gran's." It was the only place she could count on a welcome. The knowledge twisted and turned inside her. A couple of months ago, she'd possessed lots of friends. She was popular. How quickly things changed.

Fletch and Liam were doing that silent-guy-communication thing again. The silence lengthened, an uneasy one on her part. Finally, she couldn't stand the hush any longer. She pushed to her feet and walked over to the phone. She picked it up and dialed her grandmother. After a quick conversation, she hung up.

"I'm going to pack an overnight bag," she said into the silence. When neither man spoke, she turned and fled.

Liam appeared in the doorway of her bedroom a few minutes later. "You've had a rough day and you shouldn't drive. I'll take you to your grandparents' place when you're ready."

She thought about protesting but the firm set of his mouth told her he wouldn't take no for an answer. "Thanks. I won't be long."

FLETCH WAS PROWLING THE kitchen when Liam returned from taking Gaby to her grandparents. "I can't believe you let her run away."

"She needs time to decompress."

"She could do that here," Fletch snapped. "I thought we were on the same page about this. You. Me. Gaby."

"I'm not walking away from Gaby or you." Liam grabbed Fletch as he stalked past and hauled him to a stop. "No bloody way am I walking away after all the crap we've been through together. Gaby won't give up on us either, not after she's had a chance to think about things."

"What do we do now?" Fletch snarled, yanking away to stride to the far wall. He turned back, his glare flashing a warning.

"Simple. We go and visit Rachel's father tomorrow and, meantime, we have each other."

Fletch straightened. "I thought you might want to sleep in your own room tonight."

Liam grinned, his heart thumping when Fletch's usual cockiness returned to his expression. "Why would I do that when we'll have more fun together in your bed?"

"Good point." Fletch prowled closer, a glint in his eyes.

"Someone to warm my feet."

A rumbling growl worked up Fletch's throat seconds before he grasped Liam's shoulders and pulled him in for a kiss.

Liam laughed "You're easy."

"Where you and Gaby are concerned."

The amusement died in Liam. "Fancy an early night?" A spurt of surprise crossed Fletch's face and Liam smirked.

"I thought..." He shrugged.

"You thought what?"

Fletch swallowed, glanced away. "I thought we might need Gaby to bind us together."

"We still need Gaby but there's no reason why you and I can't be together or you and Gaby or me and Gaby."

Fletch remained serious but he slid his arms around Liam and tugged him into his embrace. "I'm glad. I've loved you for a long time. I don't want to lose you now."

Liam tightened his arms around Fletch, enjoying the flex of muscles beneath his fingers. He pressed a kiss to Fletch's neck then nipped lightly. "I love you too." He pulled back and grabbed Fletch's hand. "Let's go to bed."

In Fletch's bedroom, they raced to rip off their clothes. Fletch won, but only because he wasn't wearing shoes. They fell onto the bed, laughing and wrestling, their naked bodies rubbing together.

Liam hissed when their cocks brushed. Suddenly the playfulness went out of them. They stared at each other, their chests heaving. "I want you to fuck me."

"But...are you sure?"

"I trust you. I love you and I want to be together in all ways."

"You really sure? You haven't done it before." Fletch's words held clear doubt.

"You know I haven't. But we've both taken women this way. It's the same process."

"I guess," Fletch said. "We've both tried Gaby's toys. That wasn't so bad."

"I want to show you I'm committed to us," Liam said finally. "This is the only way I can think of showing you. Actions speak louder than words."

They stared at each other, and Liam's stomach roiled. He raised his hand to cup Fletch's cheek before leaning closer to kiss him. This time was slow and easy and had none of the frantic pace. It was as if they were taking time to explore each other, really learn and savor the experience. Liam flicked his tongue over Fletch's lips. Fletch opened for him and Liam slid his tongue inside. His fingers trailed lower to Fletch's jaw and stroked over the rapid tic of his pulse point. Lazily, he rocked his hips, skidding the head of his cock over Fletch's belly.

Being with Fletch was different than a woman. He didn't feel as if Fletch was judging his performance and he just went with the flow. "Tell me what you want. Tell me where you want me to touch."

"Everywhere," Fletch said, his words a warm breath of air across his jaw.

"Oh, that's real helpful."

Fletch's eyes opened and he grinned with lazy charm. "Smart-arse, what would you say?"

Liam hesitated then went for it. "I'd want you to kiss me, tug on my nipples until they sting. I'd like you to take my dick into your mouth and finger me, getting me ready for your cock. And when your mouth isn't too busy you can talk dirty to me."

"You like dirty talk?"

"I don't know. I want to find out."

Fletch chuckled and rolled without warning, placing him on top of Liam, looking down at him. "You want me to shove my cock up your ass?" His eyes glittered with arousal. "You want me to fuck you?"

"Yeah," Liam muttered, heat suffusing his cheeks. His cock jerked at the idea.

Fletch reached over to grab the lube and another of Gaby's experimental condoms. After a quick glance at the code—Gaby had trained them both—Fletch tossed them by Liam's head.

"Remember when we were talking about seducing Gaby, before she came to us with the idea of testing products for her?"

"Yeah."

"Well, at the same time I was trying to work out how to get you in bed without losing our friendship. I can't believe you're actually here and telling me you want me."

"Believe it." Liam understood Fletch's tentative manner. He felt the same way, but there was also the happiness that made him want to smile, despite the bigotry from some of the locals.

Fletch ran a hand down Liam's back and skimmed a finger between his buttocks. A jolt of pleasure struck him when Fletch pressed against his pulsing entrance. He flexed the muscles of his rump, the intrusion of Fletch's finger hard enough to spike a spear of pleasure through him.

"You feel my finger?"

"Yes," Liam whispered.

"My cock will push past that ring of muscles soon. I'll slide right inside you, and once you're good and used to me, I'll thrust until we both come. Tomorrow your arse will probably feel a bit tender."

"Do it," Liam said.

"Soon. I promise." Fletch paused. "Do you think Gaby is okay? Do you think she'll come back to us?"

"I know she loves us. It might take time, but we'll go ahead with our plan to woo her. She can't resist us." A good plan.

Fletch kissed Liam, taking it slow, although Liam sensed the urgency simmering in the depths of him. He pressed a trail of kisses down Liam's neck. One finger strummed over a flat nipple while he licked the other, giving him a hint of teeth. He played and explored until Liam's cock ached, the gleam of pre-come painting his stomach. Fletch reached in front of him to fist Liam's shaft. He handled

Liam without hesitation, his grip firm and deft. Up and down until Liam couldn't concentrate on anything except the proficient hand shoving him toward climax. His breathing turned harsh, his muscles locked and he pushed back against Fletch's chest.

"I'll come if you keep that up," Liam said with a groan when Fletch's hand caught a sensitive spot.

"That's the idea." A smile simmered in his tone and he lowered his head to suck a bite on Liam's neck. The sharp pain when he added teeth shot straight to Liam's balls. Another downward pump of Fletch's hand and Liam lost it. He came in hard spurts while Fletch's arms enveloped him in heat.

Before he could catch his breath, Fletch nudged his legs apart. The lube bottle squeaked a fraction then cool lube washed across his entrance. Liam relaxed as Fletch stretched him, the graze of a finger across his prostate swirling sparks of pleasure through him.

A sliver of unease worked through his gut, but he shoved his trepidation away, consciously relaxing as Fletch removed his fingers and ripped the condom out of its protective covering. Fletch wouldn't hurt him, not on purpose, and Liam suspected his friend would want Liam to do him in the near future. He sucked in a breath and let it ease out.

"Tell me if this hurts too much and I'll stop."

Liam nodded and attempted to remain relaxed. Fletch's mouth brushed his ear and Liam shivered, his trepidation laced with excitement too. Fletch pressed his cock against him and pushed inside a fraction. He pulled back and slipped inside Liam again.

"You feel great. Tight. Hot." Fletch nibbled his neck. "So good."

"Feels okay."

"Only okay?" Fletch reached around to stroke his cock, gripping it in one hand, sliding his fingers up and down while he burrowed deeper into Liam.

Despite his recent climax, Liam moaned, his hips pushing back against Fletch. A fine sheen of sweat coated him now, Fletch increasing the friction on Liam's cock. Fire and chills ran through his body, and when Fletch hit the right spot, every part of Liam lit up in anticipation.

"You don't have to take things so slow," Liam said, not sure whether to shove his pelvis forward into Fletch's hand or push back to take more of Fletch's cock. Excitement rocked him as pleasure started to build, layer upon layer.

"You're not sore?"

Liam chuckled, choosing to push back and force Fletch's dick deeper inside him. "You've got skills, man." Right choice. The pressure and heat combined, taking him to the fine edge of pain. An ache that felt good. So good. "Aw, hell. Fletch, don't go slow. That feels great."

Fletch took him at his word, moving with confidence and no longer holding back. "You feel perfect on this end too." His thrusts became erratic, his breathing hoarse. "Liam," he whispered.

His kiss hit Liam's neck, another on his shoulder. Then his climax burst over him, taking him by surprise. This wasn't as intense as the first one but still sweet.

Fletch cursed softly in his ear, and Liam felt the pulse of his lover's cock in his channel. Finally he stilled, pressing against Liam's back. "That was amazing. Thanks for trusting me."

"Anytime." A wave of love swept Liam. All these years he'd known Fletch—worked and played with him yet he'd never felt closer to him than he did right now.

Chapter Fourteen

GABY POPPED TWO SLICES of bread into the toaster and settled back on the stool at the breakfast counter. Her grandmother poured two cups of coffee and took possession of one of the other barstools.

"I said I'd meet Alice at the cafe," Gran said. "We're going to talk about our float for the Christmas parade. Do you want to come with me?"

After several hours of sleep Gaby actually felt better, although anyone looking at her probably wouldn't say the same. Her black eye was a beauty and certainly attention-grabbing, the bruise covering her eye and spreading down to her cheekbone. "Sure, but I thought you'd already discussed the parade at the board meeting."

"Huh!" Gran rolled her eyes. "The men wanted to toss condoms. That would really make us popular. Alice and I are nailing down the final details. Katarina would have been there but her daughter's baby is due and she promised she'd be on hand to babysit."

In the light of day, Gaby decided she wasn't going to run away, despite the sliver of anxiety in the pit of her stomach. The locals could chuck as many tomatoes at her as they liked. She'd spend the day with her grandmother and return to Liam and Fletch later this afternoon. She'd made a commitment to them. Walking away at the first setback was cowardly.

Yep, in the early hours when the morning chorus of the birds had woken her, she'd decided she couldn't let other people rule her life. So what if they didn't like the idea of a committed threesome. Too bad.

Her life.

Her right to choose how she lived it.

Alice was already at the cafe when they arrived and had taken possession of a corner table with a view of the entire place. Festive decorations and the rocking beat of a modern Christmas carol added to the usual ambience.

"Cripes," Gaby said, sliding onto a chair and nervously watching the reaction of the other customers. "Why don't we just stake out a goldfish bowl?"

"You haven't done anything wrong," Alice said in a defiant tone. "And you have a black eye because of stupid women with a pack mentality. Does your eye hurt?" Alice took her hand and squeezed it. "Are you okay?"

"There were a couple of men present, but I'm not sure if they tossed tomatoes," Gaby said, wanting to be fair on her sex.

"Your mother just came in with your sister," Gran said.

Gaby turned her head and forced a smile while inside some of her morning confidence shriveled. To her surprise, her mother saw her and changed direction, heading for their table.

"I heard about yesterday," her mother said, frowning at Gaby's black eye as she juggled several parcels wrapped in bright red paper. "Are you all right?"

"I'm fine." In truth the incident had shaken her, which was why she'd run out on Fletch and Liam.

"It's your own fault," her sister said. "You're lucky those cult women haven't sued you from what I hear."

Great! The gossip vine was alive and working well in Sloan.

"Elsa," Gaby's mother said. "That's a terrible thing to say. It's lucky her injuries weren't much worse. Look at her eye. And she's got bruises on her arms. I can only imagine how many bruises she has beneath her clothes."

"You would side with her," Elsa muttered.

"I'm not siding with anyone," her mother said. "If it were you instead of Gaby, I'd be saying the same thing."

Gaby's gaze went from Elsa to her mother and back, feeling as if she were at an interesting tennis match. Her mother was actually concerned about her.

Elsa snorted. "She's an embarrassment to our family."

"And that would be why you did the Ms. Knowall column?" Gaby asked sweetly, needled by her sister's callous attitude.

The color fled Elsa's face, surging back in a dull red tide when everyone turned to stare at her. Gaby hadn't lowered her voice. She hadn't been one hundred percent sure of her sister's guilt. Until now.

"You?" her mother said faintly. "You caused this horrid publicity for your sister? Why would you do that?"

"Jealousy," Gran said.

"I'm not jealous of Gaby. Why would I want to emulate her?"

"It doesn't matter," Gaby said. "As long as you stop, I'll forget the column ever happened."

"What about the consequences?" Gran asked, full of indignation. "She hasn't only hurt you, she's caused problems for Fletch and Liam too. She's practically ruined their business and their good names."

"Fancy Free has received free publicity," Elsa said snidely. "Besides, from what I hear Liam managed to bring this trouble down on his own head by refusing to marry

247

Rachel."

"Enough," her mother snapped. "I'm sorry, Gaby. We might not see eye to eye about many of your choices, but that doesn't mean I don't love you. I don't tell you I love you often enough." She glanced at Gran, her face softening for an instant. "It's not as if I didn't have a good example. Excuse me. We'll let you enjoy your morning coffee in peace." She grabbed Elsa's forearm and dragged her away to the far side of the cafe.

"Well, I didn't expect an apology." Gran stared after her daughter and other granddaughter. "I didn't think Elsa had the gumption to sell out her own sister."

"It doesn't matter," Gaby said, but the betrayal did trouble her. Her sister had sold her out, happily causing tension and a public backlash. A swift glance told Gaby her mother and sister were leaving. She waited until they exited the cafe and stood. "Coffee all round?"

"I'll take a latte," Gran said. "And one of Ruby's Christmas mince fruit tarts."

"A latte is fine for me," Alice said, a sympathetic smile on her face. She'd faced down a spate of gossip when she'd first arrived in Sloan and lived to tell the tale. Maybe Gaby could do the same.

Gaby headed for the counter, ordering three lattes, a mince tart, a savory scone plus some shortbread.

"Is your eye sore, love?" the elderly woman behind the counter asked. "I heard about the tomato throwing. Terrible business." Ruby made a clucking sound behind her teeth. "Although I'm thinking the UFO sightings last night will probably take precedence today. Saw the UFO myself, I did. I took the dog out for a final toilet stop before we went to bed."

"A UFO," Gaby said in a faint voice. UFOs were a hot topic in Sloan for a while but there hadn't been much activity for the last year.

"Yes, I saw the UFO as plain as day. A silver disc floated above Sloan then drifted over Ted's wheat fields before disappearing over the hills. I watched it for about five minutes."

"Did anyone else see it?" Local rumor said Ruby and her husband liked to drink homemade wine. Perhaps she'd been imbibing last night.

Gaby handed over a fifty-dollar note and waited for her change.

Another customer rushed up beside her. "Did you see the UFO last night? I did. It was amazing and just as I imagined a UFO. People all over Sloan are talking about the sighting."

Gaby grinned and accepted her change. With any luck, the UFO sightings would bury her private life under public speculation about little green men and the usual Christmas mayhem.

"What put the grin on your face?" Alice asked.

"Everyone is bursting with news about a UFO sighting last night."

"I heard someone mention sightings," Gran said. "I didn't realize it was last night."

The cafe door opened and closed, attracting Gaby's attention. "Great. Just great," she muttered on seeing the new arrival was Rachel.

"I'm shocked she has the balls to appear in public," Gran said, surprising a laugh out of Gaby. Of course, her chuckle attracted Rachel's attention. The woman froze in place for seconds, her face blanching when she met Gaby's gaze.

Rachel's breasts rose and fell when she took a deep breath. Then she surprised the hell out of Gaby by heading for their table. "I'm sorry about last night. It was my fault," she confessed rapidly, her gaze flickering over Gaby's black eye. "I threw the first tomato. I...I'm sorry." Rachel turned and fled.

"It seems a black eye works on guilty consciences." Alice winked at Gaby. "Now that we've done the true confessions, can we start work on the float plans? I'm thinking of doing a Santa's workshop. We can tie that into our new product plans and use our *Christmas is Coming* slogan without being too in your face and upsetting people."

Gran stared in the direction of Rachel's departure. "Her baby bump is bigger than I'd expect."

They paused while a young girl delivered their coffees and food.

"I like the idea," Gran said, shifting her attention to her mince tart. "We can have a Christmas tree. Get Ben or Joseph to dress as Santa Claus."

"Get some children to dress up as elves," Gaby suggested.

Alice nodded. "Exactly my thoughts. Nothing too expensive or difficult to put together. I'd like to toss some sort of favors to the crowd. Any suggestions?"

"Tomatoes," Gaby said promptly. "They're the perfect Christmas color. I volunteer to toss them."

Alice made a choking sound while her Gran cackled with delight.

"Good one, Gaby," Gran said, wiping tears of mirth from her face.

"All right, what about chocolate coins? You know the ones that come in gold-colored foil?" Gaby asked.

"They might melt if it's a hot day," Gran said. "I vote for candy canes, preferably in the red and green colors we're using in our promotion."

"Why don't we toss off some numbered discs and redeem them for special prizes? We could do a couple of adult prizes and some for the kids." Gaby chuckled without warning. "I'd like to stick it to the locals and rub their noses in condoms and sex toys."

"I love it," Alice said, smirking back at Gaby. She jotted rapid notes on a page of her notebook. She made one final note and closed her book, placing it inside her handbag. "That was easy."

"I keep telling you the men are a distraction," Gran said tartly, although her brown eyes twinkled.

"Liam and Fletch are making toy trains to sell at the farmers' market. Maybe they would lend you some to use on the float," Gaby said.

"That's a great idea. Maybe they could give us some pieces of wood so it looks as if our elves are building toys," Alice added.

"I'll ask them," Gaby said.

"Are you going home again?" Gran popped a bite of shortbread into her mouth and chewed while she regarded Gaby.

"Of course I'm going home. I was tired and upset last night. I needed to think."

"Glad to hear it," Gran said. "I like those two boys. They're decent young men and you've seemed happier lately. You need someone outside of Fancy Free. Marc wasn't right for you."

"You knew?" Gaby asked in a faint voice.

"About Marc? Of course. I'm old not stupid."

FLETCH PULLED UP IN front of Robert Saunders' house. "Are you sure this is a good idea?"

"Nope." Liam patted Fletch's thigh, smiling at Fletch's sharp intake of breath. "But I'm sick of hiding out. Let's do this." He climbed out of Fletch's SUV and marched up the path leading to Robert's imposing house. He leaned on the doorbell, hearing the faint echo of a classical song inside.

Robert answered the door. "What do you want? Have you come to your senses at last?"

Robert's smug tone made Liam want to hit him. Fletch's solid presence at his side calmed Liam and he forced his anger aside. He needed to remain composed to get through this conversation. "Can we come inside?"

Robert stood aside to let them enter.

It was an imposing entranceway with high ceilings. A spotlight highlighted a large bronze sculpture of a Madonna figure while a vase of pink peonies lent their delicate fragrance.

Robert led them into a formal reception room, no doubt meant to intimidate them. A tasteful seasonal arrangement sat on a low table, but that was the only concession to Christmas. While it wasn't what Liam was used to, he knew Fletch would feel right at home, making Liam calm by extension. He sucked in a slow breath and waited.

"Take a seat," Robert said.

"Thanks, but this won't take long." Nerves swirled through him for an instant. What if Robert still didn't believe him? He'd already damaged their business and if it wasn't for Gaby's suggestion to make toys and do up furniture they'd be struggling to pay their bills. He glanced at Fletch. His lover gave an imperceptible nod, his calm demeanour lending Liam strength.

There was no easy way to say this, so he decided to just spit it out. "I'm not going to marry Rachel, no matter how much pressure you put on me."

"You'd let a child of yours grow up like you did?" Robert mocked. "Without two parents?"

Low blow. Fletch stiffened at his side and Liam shot him a quick glance to let him know he was okay. It was true. He was the product of a teenage pregnancy, except his mother hadn't had the same support as Rachel would have from her family. His mother had done her best but she'd resented him.

"I wouldn't wish my upbringing on any child," Liam said. "If this is my child, I will support him."

"If?" Robert barked, his face turning red. "You slept with my daughter."

The front door opened and closed and footsteps approached them.

"Daddy—" Rachel broke off abruptly when she noticed Liam. She swallowed, one hand creeping up to hold her belly.

Liam stared, and he felt Fletch tense beside him. Jesus, her baby bump was huge. He calculated swiftly in his head and frowned.

"Daddy, I have something to tell you," Rachel said.

"Can't it wait?"

Rachel shot another glance at Liam and edged toward her father. "No."

"Liam's not gonna hit you," Fletch said in disgust. "He would never strike a woman."

"Liam isn't the father of my baby," Rachel blurted.

"What?" Robert demanded.

Sheer relief hit Liam and he turned to grin at Fletch. Fletch moved closer and tugged him into a quick embrace.

"You lied?" Robert demanded again, this time hoarsely

as if the fight had escaped him. "You lied about a serious matter like a baby?" His words built in pitch, almost hitting a roar.

Rachel flinched but, to her credit, stood her ground. "I'm sorry." She turned beseeching eyes on Liam. "I'm really sorry, Liam. You've always been decent to me. I was scared."

Robert glared at his daughter. "Who is the father?"

"Bryce Scott."

"That no-hoper," her father spat.

Rachel flinched again and, for an instant, Liam felt sorry for her.

"We'll go," Liam said.

Fletch scowled at Robert. "We expect you to clear Liam's name."

"Of course," Robert said. "Send me your quote and I'll take a look at it."

"I don't think so." Liam maintained a steady gaze.

Robert gave a nervous laugh. "Don't be like that. This was an easy mistake to make."

"You didn't have to behave like an ass," Fletch shot back. "You had us blackballed."

"I'll fix that today."

"We'd appreciate you spreading the word." Liam grabbed Fletch's arm and dragged him from the reception room.

Outside, Fletch shook off Liam's grasp. "We're not doing any building work for that arsehole again."

"No argument here. Once he puts the word out, we should be right for work again. Although I'd like to keep up with the toys and furniture we've been doing. I've enjoyed the change."

Fletch nodded, and despite their location, he took Liam into his arms and gave him a quick kiss. "We make a great team. Now all we have to do is get Gaby back."

"Things will be easier now that Rachel has owned up to the truth." At least that's what Liam hoped.

They drove home, a sense of relief filling Liam.

"I feel like celebrating."

Fletch indicated a right turn. "As long as I'm included in the celebration."

"Always. Both you and Gaby." He glanced out the window and let out a startled curse. "Fuck, am I seeing things?"

Fletch peered in the direction he pointed. "If it was night, I'd think I'd drunk too much," he said, screeching to a stop on the side of the road.

They both climbed out of the car and stared at the silver disc flying over Sloan. From their position above the town, they could hear the quiet whir of the motor or whatever flying saucers used to propel themselves through the sky. The UFO circled the town once before heading over Ted Morrison's wheat fields and disappearing from sight.

Fletch turned to Liam, a huge grin on his face. "Somehow I think a UFO might knock our personal lives off the pages of the *Sloan Gazette*."

"You're not wrong. What say we try our hand at some UFO toys to sell at the market? They'll sell like hotcakes."

GABY ARRIVED HOME EARLY evening after helping Alice and James decorate the flatbed truck for the parade. By the time she left, their float appeared sparkly and Christmas-like with the Christmas tree and the toy theme. The local kids would love their version of Santa's workshop. A final hour of tweaking and the pine tree added, the float would be ready for the parade in two weeks' time.

She walked into the kitchen, sniffing appreciatively at the roast chicken scent wafting through the room. As usual, Fletch and Liam were working side by side, although when she paused in the doorway, she caught them in the midst of a kiss.

"That makes me very hot," she purred. "I love seeing the

two of you together."

"Gaby!" Fletch reached her side first. He seized her in a tight hug before passing her over to an impatient Liam.

Liam ran the back of his knuckles gently over her bruised cheek and peered at her eye. "You're looking very colorful. Are you okay?"

"I'm good." Her lips curled into an impish grin. "People take one look at me and start apologizing."

"So they should," Fletch said with a growl.

"Who apologized?" Liam asked.

"My mother. Rachel. Mrs. Lisbon."

"Mrs. Lisbon, the school teacher?" Fletch demanded.

"She apologized on behalf of her teenage daughter. She was mortified when she saw me. Did you hear about the UFO? Everyone's talking about it."

"We saw the UFO this morning," Liam said, shaking his head in disbelief. "We watched it fly over the town and disappear over the hill."

"Never mind the UFO," Fletch said. "Are you back? Is everything okay with us?"

"Yes," Gaby said. "Now it's my turn to say I'm sorry. I was tired and still in shock last night. I didn't mean to reject either of you, but I needed time alone."

Liam kissed her forehead, smiling gently at her. "We hoped that was the case. We love you. We're serious about this, about you."

"There will be other times when people reject us. Are you gonna be okay with their behavior?" Fletch asked.

"I came to the same conclusion," Gaby confessed. "We haven't chosen an easy road. I'm sure there'll be times when I'll become upset and angry because of other people's reactions. But I'd feel worse without you both in my life. I'll take the bad along with the good."

"Fletch and I want children at some stage."

"So do I. We can deal with kids too when the time comes. I figure if we act embarrassed people will have cause to talk. Confidence goes a long way when you're dealing with idiots."

Fletch barked out a laugh. "True."

"Rachel admitted she lied about me being the father of her baby," Liam said.

Gaby frowned. "I thought her belly was large. Who's the father?"

"Bryce Scott." Fletch walked to the fridge and grabbed a bottle of wine plus two beers. He poured a glass for Gaby and handed drinks to both her and Liam.

"What about your work?"

Fletch and Liam exchanged a glance before Liam answered. "Robert said he'd pass around the word and lift the ban on us. He told us to send in our quote and he'd look at it."

"The man's an ass-hat," Gaby snapped.

Fletch grinned. "We practically told him the same thing. We won't be doing any work for him in the future."

"Did you tell him that?"

"Yep," Liam said with satisfaction. "We won't give him the opportunity to screw around with our livelihood again."

"Dinner is almost ready," Fletch said. "What do you say to dinner and a movie before heading to bed?"

Gaby winked at Liam. "Skip the movie part and you're on."

Chapter Fifteen

The day before Christmas

"ARE YOU SURE WE can get this tree into the living room, Gaby?" Fletch stared at the pine tree they'd purchased at the farmers' market.

"We have high ceilings," Gaby said. "The tree will fit with a couple of feet to spare." She hoped. It was a beautiful tree with evenly spaced branches. The pine scent would fill the house, and she couldn't wait to decorate the tree later that evening. This was their first Christmas together as a committed threesome and she wanted to start making strong traditions.

Liam grunted as he and Fletch dragged the tree off the trailer. "Did you measure the doorway?" He paused to wipe the sweat off his brow.

Not surprising, considering they were in the midst of an

early heat wave. The pohutukawa trees were in full bloom, their scarlet flowers heralding the Christmas season. The weather forecasters promised a hot and fine Christmas day. She, Fletch and Liam were joining James and Alice and spending the day with Richard Morgan, his wife Hinekiri as well as Luke and Janaya. They'd decided to stop in briefly to visit their families, but to spend the majority of the day with their friends.

"We'll have to take the tree through the terrace doors out the front."

Fletch rolled his eyes. "The royal 'we'."

"Aren't there three of us?" Gaby asked in an innocent tone. "Correct grammar makes that we."

Liam snorted. "There's only one of her and we still lose."

Fletch winked at him. "Yeah but what a way to go."

"I'll tell you what," Liam said. "Once we get the tree in place, we'll go down to the river for a swim."

"Skinny dipping?" Fletch asked hopefully.

Gaby smirked. "As long as no one else is there at the same time."

Liam winked at Fletch. "And we'll have a hot threesome when we get back."

"Agreed," Gaby said.

"How was I meant to know James and Alice liked the swimming hole too?" Liam groused.

"It didn't matter," Gaby said, standing back to admire the twinkling lights on their tree. She picked up the empty boxes that had stored the Christmas decorations and dropped them by the door. "We had a nice picnic with good company."

"Are we finished?" Liam asked.

Gaby turned off the main light to better admire the Christmas lights and decorations. "Yes." The tree filled the entire corner, the star on the top just scraping the ceiling. The scent of pine filled the room, mingling with the clove and cinnamon scent of the candles she'd lit earlier. It was perfect.

"Good," Fletch growled, seconds before he seized Gaby and flung her over his shoulder. "Liam and I have a private celebration in mind."

Gaby chuckled. Liam walked behind them and his shorts didn't look very comfortable. "We have a lot to celebrate. The Christmas is Coming vibrators are selling past our expectations."

"That's great, sweetheart," Fletch said. "But that's not what I had in mind." He tossed her on the bed and started yanking at her clothes. In no time flat, she was naked, her two men staring down at the bed, their eyes glittering with arousal.

Deciding to tease them, Gaby parted her legs and flashed her pussy. With one hand she played with a nipple while the other snaked between her legs to caress her clit.

Liam groaned. "I love watching you."

Fletch ripped off his T-shirt and scrambled from the rest of his clothes. He pounced like a cat, holding her hips firmly while he teased her with his lips and tongue. Already her body was moist and ready for them, the subtle teasing she'd indulged in during the afternoon like a double-edged sword. She wanted a cock inside her—heck, make that two—as soon as possible.

The mattress depressed when Liam joined Fletch and together they licked her pussy, taking turns to massage her clit. Sometimes, they backed off to kiss each other, knowing the sight made her even hotter.

When she shuddered, out of control, so close to the edge it was almost painful, they stopped.

"You know teasing is bad," she complained.

"Yeah and payback is a bitch. You and Liam ganged up on me last night," Fletch said.

"Take the torture like an adult."

"Hell, listen to him," Gaby said, sharing a speaking glance with Fletch. "He isn't listening to us cautioning about revenge."

"I'm listening," Liam said, reaching over to grab the lube. "You two can gang up on me anytime. I'm yours to command. What position do you want?"

"Gaby on her hands and knees. I'm not gonna last long this time. Gaby can suck me off while you take her. Besides, we have the entire night to drive her crazy."

Gaby rose with alacrity, turning onto her hands and knees and waggling her butt. "Enough with the talk. I don't need you guys. I have my trusty vibrator and attachments."

"But you want us," Fletch said, unperturbed. He slapped her on the bottom when he noticed her hand reaching toward her clit for a furtive stroke.

"And you love us." Liam smeared a little of the pleasure-enhancing lube on his cock.

Gaby looked over her shoulder, smiling in acceptance. Nothing less than the truth. She'd never felt happier. She sighed when she felt Liam line up his cock, pushing her butt back against him to take him deeper. At the tap of Fletch's cock against her lips, she opened her mouth and took him inside. The musky flavor of him burst across her taste buds, and she swirled her tongue across his sweet spot, wanting more.

Liam pushed deep, filling her before withdrawing. Evidently he was feeling on edge too because he reached beneath her to finger her clit. Gaby shivered. She let her mind drift, surrendering to the pleasure swirling inside both body and mind. Clued in to the signs of imminent explosion by both her men, she increased her suction on Fletch and tightened her inner muscles around Liam.

Liam pulled back and thrust into her hard, nudging her over into orgasm. The sweet sensations roared through her body. Her pussy spasms gripped Liam and he groaned in enjoyment. Seconds later, Fletch came in her mouth and she concentrated on him. She licked him gently until he pushed her away. Liam pulled out of her and they fell together in a tangle of limbs.

Gaby sighed in contentment and snuggled up to her men. Christmas was definitely coming.

THANK YOU FOR READING *Romp*. Did you enjoy it? If so, please consider leaving a review at your favorite online bookstore. A review would make my day!

Curious about the UFO sightings in this story? All the answers to your questions can be discovered in *Janaya*, Luke and Janaya's romance, (www.shelleymunro.com/books/janaya) or in *Hinekiri*, Richard and Hinekiri's romance. (www.shelleymunro.com/books/hinekiri)

Please turn the page for an excerpt from *Buzz*, the next story in the *Fancy Free* series.

Excerpt – Buzz

"Sebastian."

A sharp elbow to Sebastian Lang's ribs jerked him off balance and he almost head-butted his date. He grasped her upper arms before she toppled on her butt in a chain reaction. "Sorry, sweetheart." He made sure she was okay before scowling at his friend Wayne, who hovered beside them. "What did you do that for?"

Wayne pantomimed something, frustration knitting his brow when Sebastian stared at him blankly. He tried again, his face screwing up until his expression resembled a tribal mask carved by one of his Māori ancestors. Obviously whatever Wayne wanted to say wasn't fit for a woman's ears.

"It's okay," the attractive blonde cooed, a heavy coating of mascara aiding her slow, sexy blink. "I'll give you some privacy 'cause I have to visit the little girls' room anyway."

Sebastian fought to restrain his grimace. *The little girls' room. Really?* Why didn't she call it a toilet and leave it at that? Everyone had to take a piss sometime. She waggled her fingers in a coy wave and sashayed away—or as much as she could sway wearing her tight little skirt and skyscraper heels.

"Sebastian!"

"What?" Sebastian glared at his longtime friend and business partner Wayne Garrett.

Wayne tore his gaze off the dance floor to study him properly. "What's crawled up your arse tonight?"

Nothing Wayne could fix. "What do you want?"

Wayne leaned closer, his tanned face alight with mischief. "Do you still have your remote control for the Fancy Free vibrator?"

"Not on me. It's in the office."

"Too bad. I persuaded Jocelyn to wear the vibrator tonight and noticed something interesting when I used the remote. Go and ask Jen for a dance."

Sebastian's brows rose. "Our Jen?"

Wayne grinned with his entire face. "I forgot that you haven't seen her yet. See the woman with the long, straight brown hair? The one wearing the short black skirt and pink top?"

Whoa! Nice arse. "That's Jen Alexander?"

"She cleans up good, huh? You should have seen her in shorts this morning. Made me feel way better about stopping by her house to pick up paperwork. I had no idea she was hiding that luscious body beneath her navy-blue suit."

"Stop." Sebastian held up his hand to enforce the harsh note in his voice. "That's Jen you're lusting over. She works for us and that makes her out of..." He trailed off, realizing what his friend was getting at. This was Jen's leaving party. After years of nursing her mother then working long hours to save money, she was going back to school full-time.

"Go and ask her to dance."

"Where's Giles? And where is Jocelyn?"

Wayne's face hardened, ice freezing his former humor. "Libby told me the bastard sent her a breakup text five minutes before she left for the party."

"A text? Prick better not come near me when we're working with Liam and Fletch's crew next week," Sebastian said with a growl. "And Jocelyn?"

"Jocelyn is in the kitchen talking to her cousin. Go before your date comes back from the *little girls' room*."

"You heard."

"Yep. You don't want her in your bed, Seb."

No, he didn't. He wanted Wayne. Sebastian shoved the thought aside, locking it firmly away and headed for Jen.

SHELLEY MUNRO

Thoughts like that had no business popping into his mind. Sighing, he weaved through the crowds of employees and friends on the dance floor. Laughter filled the Sloan town hall and the scent of hot sausage rolls floated on the air with the Women's Division matriarchs in the thick of the kitchen action.

"Jen?" Sebastian tapped her on the shoulder. "Would you like to dance?"

Jen turned and Sebastian got his first look at the miraculous transformation of their junior office assistant. Her curly hair no longer hung in uncontrolled chaos around her face. She must have visited a hairdresser because now it was dead straight and the shiny brown mass tumbled down her back. Her clothes were different too, showcasing a curvy body. Even her features looked different with an expert application of makeup.

"You look gorgeous, Jen." Not even her slightly reddened blue eyes detracted from her natural beauty. "Those high school boys aren't going to know what hit them."

"See! I told you." Gaby Montgomery, one of Jen's friends, sent her a thumbs-up.

Jen grinned, making her look more like the familiar Jennifer of the office. "I'm not going to school to check out the boys. I'm going to study. Besides, they're all at

272

least seven years younger than me. When I date, I want a man—" She broke off suddenly, her good humor faltering, and Sebastian wanted to beat Giles to a pulp for hurting her.

He grabbed her hand. "Come and dance with me."

Jen found herself tugged into the midst of friends strutting their stuff on the floor. Sebastian put his arms around her, holding her lightly as they moved to the melody.

"We're going to miss you around the office."

"I'll still help Libby during my holidays." Somehow she didn't think Sebastian and Wayne would miss her in quite the same way she'd miss them. Her bosses were both sexy men and in high demand with the single women living in and around the country town of Sloan. Local rumor said they'd used their building skills to install revolving doors on their bedrooms.

Not that she'd know. They treated her like a younger sister—which was as it should be, she reminded herself. Mind back on the plan.

Finish school. Accounting degree.

She didn't have time for a man in her life.

"That's good to hear." Sebastian smiled at her, ice blue eyes crinkling at the corners. "You know if you need anything all you have to do is ask."

"Thanks. I—" She broke off with a surprised gasp.

"What is it? What's wrong?"

"N-nothing," she said in a strangled voice. The new Fancy Free vibrator, the remote-controlled one she'd promised to test for her inventor friend Gaby, buzzed to life again. The very one she'd inserted minutes before Giles had so kindly sent her a text dumping her arse, vibrated on the perfect spot. She bit her bottom lip, concentrating on holding back her gasps of enjoyment. That felt *sooo* good.

The vibrations ceased as suddenly as they'd started. Thank god! That had been the second time tonight. She sucked in a hasty breath and glanced around for Giles. No, she was pretty sure he wasn't here. But she would be demanding back the remote control the second she saw the louse.

If he thought he could wriggle back into her good graces, he was sadly mistaken. No one treated her like a doormat and got away with it. And as soon as this dance ended, she'd make a hasty trip to the restrooms. If Gaby hadn't hustled her out of the house so quickly she'd have removed the vibrator before she'd left home. Since arriving at the hall, she hadn't managed a quiet moment to herself.

"What made you decide to change your hair?" Sebastian asked.

Jen frowned. Had he noticed her weird behavior?

"Jen?"

Oh dear. He would if she didn't act normally. "Libby gave me a voucher for the new beauty spa. Gaby dragged me off this afternoon and paid for a visit to the hairdresser."

"Giles is a fool."

"You heard?" Her gaze flew to his before flitting away in embarrassment. She didn't want his sympathy.

"Jen, look at me." His imperious tone brooked no refusal and his callused fingertips tipping her face upward sealed the deal. "You're better off without the idiot."

The insistent buzz in her pussy started again. She groaned, saw his eyes widen and suspicions start to coalesce.

"What else did Gaby give you?"

"Nothing." The stimulation intensified. Chills chased across her flesh and for one horrid moment she thought her knees would buckle. Another quick punch of heat forced a moan from her.

"Giles better not have control of that remote," Sebastian said in a snarl.

Hmmm, I wonder what happens next in this delectable threesome tale...

www.shelleymunro.com/books/buzz

About Author

USA Today bestselling author Shelley Munro lives in Auckland, the City of Sails, with her husband and a cheeky Jack Russell/mystery breed dog.

Typical New Zealanders, Shelley and her husband left home for their big OE soon after they married (translation of New Zealand speak - big overseas experience). A twelve-month-long adventure lengthened to six years of roaming the world. Enduring memories include being almost sat on by a mountain gorilla in Rwanda, lazing on white sandy beaches in India, whale watching in Alaska, searching for leprechauns in Ireland, and dealing with ghosts in an English pub.

While travel is still a big attraction, these days Shelley

is most likely found in front of her computer following another love - that of writing stories of contemporary and paranormal romance and adventure. Other interests include watching rugby (strictly for research purposes), cycling, playing croquet and the ukelele, and curling up with an enjoyable book.

Visit Shelley at her Website
www.shelleymunro.com

Join Shelley's Newsletter
www.shelleymunro.com/newsletter

Follow Shelley at Bookbub
www.bookbub.com/authors/shelley-munro

Other Books by Shelley

Fancy Free
Protection
Romp
Buzz
Festive

Friendship Chronicles
Secret Lovers
Reunited Lovers
Clandestine Lovers
Part-Time Lovers
Enemy Lovers
Maverick Lovers
Sports Lovers

Military Men
Innocent Next Door
Soldiers with Benefits
Safeguarding Sorrel
Stranded with Ella
Josh's Fake Fiancée
Operation Flower Petal
Protecting the Bride

Bundle
Military Men

Alien Encounter series
Janaya
Hinekiri
Alexandre

Bundle
Alien Encounter